Resourceful

Kari Lee Harmon

OLIVERHEBERBOOKS

Cover art by Dar Albert at Wicked Smart Designs

Published by Oliver-Heber Books

0 9 8 7 6 5 4 3 2 1

This book is dedicated to my mother, Marion Harmon, my sister, Debbie Russo, and my daughter, Emily Townsend. Three generations of a special bond that only exists between mothers, sisters, and daughters. I am so blessed and grateful to still have all of mine.

Chapter One

re·source·ful

ADJECTIVE
Having the ability to find quick and clever ways to overcome difficulties.

"The legend of the tattooed clover?" I asked above the slow, crooning Irish singer in the corner, and spilled my martini in the process.

My best friends and I sat at a wooden table by the crackling fire in the back of McGinny's Pub, celebrating. The Irish bar was a favorite of ours. The conversation this evening had turned interesting, to say the least, just as I had hoped.

Only, I had to have heard Harm wrong....

"You heard me right, Tiffany." Harmony Jones

chuckled as though she'd read my mind and then chugged her beer.

I eyed her skeptically. Harm lived to shock people—hence her red spiky hair, body piercings, and voodoo hobby—so when she talked, we took what she had to say with a grain of salt.

"I'm serious this time. Some woman came into my shop this morning, asking about all my New Age stuff. We started talking, and she filled me in on this juicy rumor." Harm paused as she met each of our eyes in turn. "I repeat. Any of you babes heard about the legend of the tattooed clover penis, or what?"

I wiped up the martini drops with a cocktail napkin, and a smile crept across my face. The girls had come through for me again. This was exactly what I needed tonight. Something outrageous enough to keep me from freaking out over getting old.

I abhorred change.

Zoe Robinson choked on her chardonnay. "Good Lord in Heaven, no," she chimed in after regaining her breath, her caramel curls bouncing off her shoulders and her amber eyes an inch wide.

It didn't take much to shock Zoe. She acted so innocent. You'd never know the darling had just had a secret affair with a younger man. He was only a few years younger, but it still counted. Harm had thrown even me for a loop this time, and I taught sensual massage for a living.

"I heard about that." Morticia Smith's dark eyes twinkled as she adjusted the knot of black silky hair at the nape of her neck.

That was about all you'd get from Morti without prodding. Growing up around a funeral home, she had always related better to the dead than the living. As her best friends, we were the exception. We knew the real her. The funny, sensitive, charming her.

"Okay, I'll bite." I held up a hand before they could say anything, because trust me, they were about to pounce on that lovely little faux pas. "Scratch that." I winced. Usually, I had a way with words, but obviously not tonight. I tried again. "What I meant to say is, what exactly is the legend of the tattooed clover penis?"

Harmony shot Morticia a pleading, hopeful look. "Do you want to do the honors, or can I?"

"The floor's all yours, Harm." Morti sat back and took a drink of her diet cola and then folded her hands in her lap.

"Yes!" Harm made a fist and punched the air. Twice. "Listen up, babes, cuz this is good." She leaned in. "Rumor has it, there's a guy in town who has a tattoo."

"A tattoo? So do you, doll. Several, in fact." I arched one eyebrow high. "And that's legend-worthy how?"

"I might have a couple tattoos, but not on my thingypoo." Harm snorted and then frowned. "Not that I have a thingypoo." She waved her hands. "Oh, hell, you get the point."

"What on earth would possess someone to do that?" Zoe cringed and shook her head. "That has to be painful."

"Wait, it gets better." Morti's mysterious and rare Mona Lisa smile played at the corners of her full lips.

"There's more?" I laughed. "What could possibly be better than a man with a tattoo on his penis?"

Harm chuckled. "The tattoo is of a four-leaf clover."

"I gathered as much," I said, pointing out, "the legend has *clover* right in the name. How are clovers legendary?"

"Because not every clover has four leaves." Morti held up a finger. "Tell them the rest of the legend, Harm."

"Well, the story goes the guy has a tattoo of a clover on his penis, but you can only see the fourth leaf if you get lucky. Meaning, you make him grow hard, he sprouts a fourth leaf." Harm burst out laughing. "Gotta admit *that* is legend-worthy."

"Oh, good God," Zoe croaked, fanning her face. "I don't believe that. Who would do such a thing?"

"That's the kicker." Harmony glanced at Morticia. "You sure you don't wanna tell them the rest, babe?"

Morti laughed. "Hell, you're on a roll, sister, take it away."

"The man with the clover is the one and only big strapping Irishman and local pub entrepreneur himself, Mr. Matthew McGinnis." Harm sat back, looking way too pleased with her little ole' self.

Meanwhile, I started to hyperventilate. I fanned my face and the firelight reflected off my rings, sending colors of the rainbow dancing across our table.

"Are you okay?" Concern puckered Zoe's forehead.

"I'm fine. Hot flash." I pulled at my neckline. It wasn't

a lie. A wave of heat had most definitely flashed through my every cell over that thought. I cleared my throat...twice. "M-Matt McGinnis you say?"

"In the flesh." Harm grinned wide. "At least I wish he was in the flesh. I'd love to take a gander at that laddy boy's shamrock."

Matthew McGinnis had moved to small town Mayflower, Massachusetts, to take over his uncle's Irish pub, and we'd been flirting ever since. He kept stopping by my massage parlor, but we always seemed to miss each other. In fact, it had been a while since I'd even seen him before tonight. The last time being at this very table when I'd celebrated the fifth anniversary of my divorce over a month ago.

A sobering thought settled into my brain. Maybe he'd lost interest. Shoving that thought to the back of my mind, I refused to believe I'd lost my touch. Maybe it was time I renewed my acquaintance with Mr. McShamrock.

"Wow, who would have thought a man like Matt would get a tattoo of any kind, let alone one there?" Zoe studied the blond giant behind the bar. "He seems so conservative, and, well...normal."

"Hey, I have tattoos. Are you saying I'm not normal?" Harm arched her auburn brows as she leaned back in her chair.

"Of course you're normal." I patted her hand. "Tattoos are great, doll, but I'm with Zoe. Matthew McGinnis does *not* seem like the kind of person who would get one like that and especially *there*."

Harmony eyed the hulk of a man as he smiled wide, his dimples sinking deep, and his animated conversation captivating everyone around him. "He looks big enough to sprout a fourth leaf to me."

"That he does." Morticia's gaze followed Harmony's, and I knew full well they were mentally devouring the massive shoulders, broad chest, and impressive bulge even I couldn't take my eyes off. "He's gonna make some woman very happy if she gets lucky enough to see that fourth leaf."

"I was born lucky," I heard myself say.

Three pairs of eyes whipped back around to lock on me. I laughed, feigning confidence, when I felt anything but. What was wrong with me? I was never this insecure.

"Do I detect a bet?" Harm asked.

Leave it to Harmony to jump on what I'd said and hold me to it. "Depends on the wager," I answered, studying my manicure as though I didn't have a care in the world.

"I got twenty bucks that says you can't put that rumor to bed." Harm's grin stretched so wide she looked like the star in a toothpaste commercial, filling me with an urge to grab a yellow sharpie and color her teeth.

"Surely you jest." I scoffed. "I simply meant I could get him to ask me out, not that I would sleep with him."

"I didn't say you had to sleep with him, but if you do, lucky you. I just want proof of the infamous clover. But, hey, if you can't handle the bet, then—"

"I can handle it just fine...literally." I matched her grin with a tilt of my chin and a raise of my brow. "But for what you're asking me to do, you'd better make it fifty."

"Deal. You've got twenty-four hours to prove if the tattoo exists or not." Harm slapped her hand on the table. "Anyone else in?"

"What the hell, I'll match her fifty." Morti tapped her fist twice on the table. "Curiosity killed the cat, and all." She shrugged.

"Well, since you did bet on me several times not very long ago, I'm in too." Zoe winced. "Sorry, Tiff, what's fair is fair."

"It's really no big deal, ladies. I just have to get Matt to ask me out and then prove the tattoo exists or doesn't exist. Piece of cake." Or at least it would have been a piece of cake before I'd lost my confidence.

Damn birthdays.

I stood and smoothed my hands down the front of my favorite periwinkle blue, strapless, silk dress in the same shade as my eyes. Fingering the diamond at my neck, I stared at Matt. Curly hair, chiseled features, and a booming laugh that made me smile every time I heard it. Renewed confidence filled me. Some simple flirting, a little conversation, and I'd have my answer, not to mention a lovely little boost to my ego.

How hard could it be?

So not going there...at least not yet.

"Ladies, I'll be right back with another round." I flipped my long blonde waves over my shoulder and focused on Matt, putting an extra swing in my step as I made my way over to the bar, ignoring the giggles behind me. I could do this. I had to, for a much-needed confidence boost.

I sidled up to the bar, untied the silk scarf around my neck, and let it drape over my shoulders. Resting my forearms on the slick, granite countertop, I leaned in just enough for the kill.

Only the kill never came.

Matt tended to every single person at the bar, keeping me waiting—I never waited—then he finally swaggered down to my end, never once lowering his gaze to my cleavage. Granted, I might not have Double Ds like Zoe, but I was a nice, respectable, solid C, dammit.

Something was very wrong with this picture.

"Ms. Eisenhower." Matt nodded. "What brings ye out this fine evening?" His deep voice sent a ripple through my stomach as though I were a cello he had just strummed, and a warm smile spread across his rugged face, heating my insides.

At least I hoped the heat was from his smile, and I wasn't experiencing my first actual hot flash. I shuddered, turning my focus back to more appealing thoughts. Matt's smile was genuine enough, but it didn't quite reach his bedroom eyes.

I toyed with a cocktail napkin, looking up at him through my lashes. "Well, doll, I'm celebrating again."

He leaned on an elbow, his bicep bulging, and arched a blond shaggy brow. "Another divorce?"

"Hardly, darling. One marriage was enough to last me a lifetime. I don't make mistakes twice."

"Good motto. I try not to make mistakes, period." He

winked, but something still felt wrong. I just couldn't put my finger on it. "So, what are ye celebrating?" he asked.

"My birthday."

"Really, now." He nodded once. "Well, happy birthday to ya, lass." He dried a wine glass, his hands looking huge against the delicate crystal, then he hung the glass from the wooden slats above the bar.

"You're not going to ask how old I am?"

He laughed a hearty boom, his green McGinny's t-shirt stretched tight across his chest, revealing the flex of his impressive pecs. "I come from a big family. I know better than that." He wiped off the counter with a rag and then slung the cloth over his shoulder. "So what can I get for ye?"

"A glass of chardonnay, whatever you have on tap, a diet cola, and a martini—shaken, not stirred." I licked my lips. "And make it dirty, would you, doll?"

"Coming right up." He moved behind the bar with such ease, looking as though he'd spent the better part of his life there. Rumor had it, he grew up in Dublin.

My gaze dropped, and I couldn't help staring at his firm gluts encased oh-so-nicely in a pair of tight-fitting jeans. I sighed, having forgotten just how hot Matt was, and the image of expanding clover tattoos and sprouting leaves danced behind my eyes.

Gracious. I tore my gaze away and sat before I fell. I had to get ahold of myself, or I'd come undone right here and now on this barstool, but I couldn't help it. The man was a living, breathing legend. I glanced at my best friends and shot them a sultry smile.

"That'll be forty dollars, please."

My smile slipped, and all I could do was turn around and gape at the man. He was charging me? Last time I was here, he'd bought the girls and me a round of drinks on the house, but now he was charging me on my birthday?

I snapped my jaw closed and forced a smile. "Um, I forgot my purse at my table."

"That's okay, I can wait." His smile never wavered. In fact, I was quite certain his dimples had deepened.

Unbelievable.

This had never happened to me, and quite frankly, I had no idea how to handle it. "Peachy." I straightened and retied my scarf, so it covered my cleavage. Why waste that on a man who obviously didn't have any taste at all. "I'll, um, be back in a sec."

I headed to our table with dread, and the Irish singer's gaze met mine as though he'd seen it all go down, his sad wailing voice vibrating beneath my Jimmy Choos. I straightened my shoulders and ignored the man who had to be related to Matt. He looked just like him. I didn't want sympathy...

I wanted justice.

"Where are the drinks? Do you need help carrying them?" Zoe glanced beyond me toward the bar.

"Oh, I've got it covered. I just forgot my purse, so I—"

"You have to pay for them?" Morti's dark brows shot up clear to her hairline. "That's gotta be a first."

"Hardly." I shrugged off her comment. But I had to admit, I'd at least expected a complimentary birthday drink for me.

"Get out." Harm gawked at me. "See what happens when you turn forty? Looks like I win. Time to pay up, babes."

"Not so fast. You haven't won anything yet, thank you very much." I snatched up my purse and marched back to the bar, ignoring the curious glances the regulars sent my way, petrified that Harmony was right. But I refused to believe that would happen.

I wouldn't allow it to happen.

I slid a fifty-dollar bill onto the bar. "Keep the tip, doll." I winked.

"Thanks. Enjoy yer birthday." Matt headed to the other end of the counter without so much as a single backward glance.

"Oh, I will, you can count on that." I picked up the tray of drinks and strolled back to our table with as much dignity as I could muster.

So, this was how crashing and burning felt. For as long as I could remember, even back in high school, I had never been shot down. With my divorce, I'd been the one to ask for it, and I got it.

This could not be happening to me.

"The day that Tiffany Eisenhower can't score is a sad day indeed. Now all hope is lost." Harm chugged her beer. "We'd better enjoy tonight cuz it's downhill from here."

"How would you know? You're not even forty yet." I

drained my martini. "And I'll have you know the last time I looked in the mirror, everything was still firmly uphill."

"Good genes will do that for you." Morti drank her diet cola. "Eventually everything heads south...or so I'm told."

"Girls, just because Tiff's forty doesn't mean her life is over." Zoe smiled dreamily. "Look what happened to me when I turned forty."

Zoe's husband of twenty years had run off, leaving her with four children to raise. But she was resilient. She'd picked herself up, made a big success of her party-planning business when she won the bid for Mayor Edward's Annual Labor Day Bash, and she'd gotten engaged to the town's hot new Hunky Dr. Chaz Anderson.

"Yeah, well, you got lucky." Harm snorted. "But it looks like Tiff won't."

"Girls, I paid for my own drinks, that's all. It's not like that's never happened before." I bit the end of the olive off, my gaze wandering back to the enigma behind the bar as though a magnet had reeled me in. "The bet's still on, and the night is still young."

Twenty-four hours...I swallowed hard.

What the hell had I gotten myself into?

Chapter Two

Midnight.

I must be getting old if I was this tired already. I'd tried all evening to engage Matt in conversation. He'd remained friendly and polite, yet never once flirted with me. Maybe I had read the signs he'd been giving me wrong. Something had changed since the last time I'd seen him, but for the life of me, I couldn't figure out what.

I couldn't go home until I won the bet, even though the girls had long since abandoned me. My pride wouldn't let me. So, I focused back on Homer—the youngest of Harmony's seven older brothers—and smiled indulgently.

He droned on and on about his prized Mustang he was souping up in his garage. He'd been hitting on me all night, but that was nothing new. He'd had a crush on me for years and was a nice enough guy—almost as big and handsome as Matt—but he did nothing for me.

Not that I wanted Matt to do anything for me, either, except maybe physically. Physical affairs, with no strings attached, were all I allowed myself. I liked my independent lifestyle too much to risk answering to another man ever again.

Tonight was about proving I still had it. And getting lucky enough to find a four-leaf clover, that's all. Not that I planned to do anything with the laddy's shamrock—as Harm would say—other than take a peek for proof purposes only.

But I wasn't at all positive whom I was trying to convince.

"Well, I'd better hit the hay. Gotta open up the garage at the crack of dawn, and then cover Harm's shop on her lunch hour. Ma needs her, as usual. Cut the cord already, right?" Homer grunted and jerked his head to the side to flip the red strands of hair out of his green eyes.

"She will when she's ready, doll," I answered, remembering exactly why he didn't do anything for me.

Homer was handsome enough, but still rough around the edges, whereas my tastes tended to run toward the more refined. An image of Matt McGinnis popped into my mind's eye. While he might be big and rugged, he had an air of worldliness and charm about him.

"It's closing time, Ms. Eisenhower," Matt's deep voice rumbled from right behind me, and I jumped. "See ya, Homer," he added.

"Later, Matt." Homer sent Matt a two-fingered salute.

"Catch you on the flipside, Tiff." He winked as he swaggered out of the bar.

"I thought you didn't close until two?" I focused my attention on Matt, who was studying me with an expression I couldn't quite read.

"That's on weekends, lass." He glanced around the interior. "It's Wednesday, and the bar's empty." His gaze landed on my silk dress with a raised eyebrow as he added, "A woman like ye must have someplace to be?" before walking to the front door and flipping the sign to *closed*, then turning the lock.

"Nope." Sad but true, I thought as I ran my finger around my empty martini glass. No date, no man...nothing.

All I had were a good-for-nothing ex who was bleeding me dry with more alimony demands, parents who didn't want me, a sister who didn't get it because she was the twin they kept, and my grandmother—the woman who raised me and the only person who ever loved me—but Grammy was losing her battle with breast cancer.

A lump formed in my throat.

I didn't know what I'd do once she was gone. I couldn't bear to think about that, so I focused on the only other thing I had going for me. My looks. A bit shallow, but true, and I worked hard to maintain them. Although based on tonight's turn of events—Homer didn't count—I was obviously losing those as well.

I sighed, glancing down at my empty glass. How many of these little lovelies did I have, anyway? It had been a long night, I thought as I stared deeply into Matt's baby blues. Not a hard task to do by any means.

His smile dimmed and a brief flash of wariness flitted across his chiseled features, but then it disappeared. "Well, I'm a wee bit tired myself. C'mon. Ye can leave through the back with me."

I followed him through the game room by the pool and poker tables and dartboard, thinking the time had come to pull out all the stops. Go for it. Give it all I had. When he reached for the handle, I put my hands on his back, feeling his muscles bunch, and noticed my head only came to his shoulders. I was five-ten.

Not too many men towered above me.

"Wait," I said on a breathy whisper, the sheer size of him overwhelming me. I had to think of something to get him to stay. So far, I'd tried everything, but nothing had worked.

He froze, his back still to me. "Ms. Eisen—"

"Tiffany. Call me Tiffany...please." Give it all I had? I blinked.

Oh, my God, I had nothin'. When the hell had that happened? The reality hammered through me. Goodness gracious, maybe I really was losing my touch. This was no longer about a stupid bet. I just wanted to feel desirable. Special. But I didn't feel special, I felt stupid. And alone.

And...old.

A lump formed in my throat. What the hell was I doing here? I really hadn't expected turning forty would hit me this hard, and it didn't help that I'd drank just enough little lovelies to make me emotional.

"Tiffany, I don't think—"

"Then d-don't think." I swallowed my sob.

He turned around slowly and dipped his head to look in my eyes. "What's wrong, lass? Are ye crying?"

And that was all it took.

"Don't be ridiculous." I rubbed my eyes, keeping the tears at bay, thank God. I hadn't cried in a man's arms in about ten years, before my ex-husband had turned into an asshole, and I didn't plan to start now. "I must have something in my eye, is all."

"Here, follow me." He took my arm and led me to the center of the room, then placed his hands on either side of my waist, his fingers nearly spanning the circumference as he lifted me onto the pool table.

"What about the felt?" I asked, startled at the turn of events. "I don't want to ruin your pool table."

"This old table has been in my family for decades. There's not much you can do that my nieces and nephews haven't already done. Besides, my uncle restores old furniture, so don't worry about it." He winked.

Well, now, this was a first. Me learning something new about men and romance. Who knew a little sincere vulnerability would work better than a peek at my girls. I decided to roll with it and continue being myself—an over-sensitive mess—but got distracted by his smell: soap, fabric softener, a touch a booze, and something uniquely...him.

"Tiffany, hello, are ye in there?" He arched a brow, his

lips quirking up at one corner, granting me a glimpse of an adorable dimple. "I said, which eye has something in it?"

"Huh...oh, um, th-the right." I cleared my throat.

He bent his knees slightly, so he was on eye level with me as he cradled my cheeks with his palms. I couldn't breathe. Something about Matt rattled me, completely throwing me off my game every time I was around him.

Tonight was no exception.

Using his thumbs to hold my eye open, he tipped my head to the left and right as he searched the depths. The blue of his eyes was so pale, it resembled the calm waters of a Caribbean tide pool on a windless day. I wanted to reach out and touch them just to see if they would ripple.

He blew a soft puff of air square in my eye, and I flinched. "Oh." I scrunched my eyes closed.

"A trick me mum taught me back in Ireland when I was a lad." The deep timber of his voice vibrated my mid-section.

I pried my eyes open in time to see him beam as though he'd performed some intricate feat like eye surgery or restoring my vision.

"Feel better?" He waited expectantly.

I squinted, my eye now irritated, given that it had nothing in it to begin with. "Much." I feigned a smile. "Thanks."

"Yer welcome." He started to lift me down, but I rested my fingertips on his corded forearms and his gaze snapped down to mine, a deep V forming between his brows.

"You come from Dublin, right?" I smiled a genuine smile, really just needing to be held. "It's a beautiful city."

A grin filled with warmth and pride replaced his frown. "Ye've been there?"

"A few times. I love the magnificent architecture, and those rolling green hills and jagged cliffs in the countryside," my hand fluttered to my bosom, "why, it's enough to take your breath away."

His gaze finally dropped to my cleavage, and I realized what I had done. My confidence building, I wiggled my fingers and his eyes widened. Oh, yeah. I still had it. I let my lids close halfway and watched him, watch me, feeling my body tingle all over in response.

"That it does," he managed, and then tore his gaze away from my breasts, giving my C cups the respect they deserved. "It's yer birthday, right?" He looked as though he were struggling for a distraction.

I nodded as I moistened my lips.

He zoomed in on the tip of my tongue, and his Adam's apple bobbed. "Being that it's after hours and I can join ye now, how about I buy ye a drink, lass?" He made a beeline for the bar, downing a shot as soon as he got there.

I bit back a giggle, feeling sooo much better. "Have any champagne? I prefer Crystal."

He arched a brow. "Ye wouldn't be what they call 'high maintenance,' would ye now?" His lips formed a slanted grin as he opened a fresh bottle. "I don't have much call for Crystal, but I do have a bottle of Dom Perignon."

"Dom will do just fine." I quirked a brow. "And if you

call having standards 'high maintenance,' then I guess I am."

"Not that there's anything wrong with that, of course." He chuckled as he poured himself a tankard of dark beer.

"Of course." I met his smile with one of my own.

He carried our drinks over to the pool table and then handed me my sparkling wine, the tiny bubbles fizzing and popping as I sipped. After hopping up beside me, he took a long draw from his beer and let out a sigh of ecstasy by the sound of it, which only succeeded in heightening my senses further.

He raised his glass. "Nothing like an ice-cold Guinness after a hard day's work."

I felt his deep voice throb in places it had no business throbbing, so I crossed my legs and leaned back on one hand as I nursed my drink with the other. "Exactly. Only I prefer martinis or champagne."

"Shaken, not stirred, and top of the line." His shoulder brushed mine as he leaned over when he spoke. "Extra dirty."

"Is there any other kind?" My smile came slow and sweet as I peeked at him from the corner of my eye. "You remembered."

He stared at me for a long moment only to pull away and softly say, "Yer not an easy woman to forget, Ms. Eisenhower."

I met his gaze full on and heat blazed between us. "You're not easy to forget, either, Mr. McGinnis." Reaching out a finger, I dipped the tip inside one of his dimples. "I've wanted to do that for so long, you have no idea."

"Glad I could accommodate ye." His smile remained in place, but he studied me with a mixture of longing and wariness.

He could accommodate me oh-so-well, but I still couldn't figure out what was holding him back. All I knew was, I wanted him more than I had ever wanted anyone. "Speaking of accommodating—"

"Oh, look at that, yer glass is nearly empty." He vaulted off the table and headed to the bar.

I glanced at my glass that was nearly full and smiled a little. I was getting to him. I looked back up at him and swallowed hard. He was getting to me, too. His fabulous glutes flexed all the way to the bar, distracting me from the fact that he was still holding out on me. Wow, what that man did to a pair of jeans was downright sinful. Thanks be to Jesus. I wasn't a religious woman by nature, but I was all about giving credit where credit was due.

God got it right when he'd created Matthew McGinnis.

Good thing my apartment was just a few doors down from his pub. Two glasses and several flirtatious conversations later, Matt said, "Well, lass, it's getting late. Let me walk ye home." He hopped off the table and stumbled a bit. Go figure, since he'd added shots to chase his beer ever since we'd started the conversation about accommodating.

"Wait, I need help," I said to his incredibly wide back.

I didn't want the night to end. He'd cheered me up, and he was so easy to talk to, it just felt good being around him.

He paused, turning around slowly. "Oh, sorry. Me Ma would have me head fer that." His brogue got thicker with every shot he'd downed. He placed his hands on my waist, but I wrapped my legs around his middle and my arms snaked around his neck as he lifted me. He froze. "Lass, ye be playing with fire, ye know."

"Aye," I said, imitating his accent with a poor version of my own. "I'm old enough to know what I be playing with, laddy."

A goofy cockeyed smile played across his face. "Do ye now?"

I let go on purpose and started to slide down his body, but his hands slid beneath my bottom, catching me just as my most intimate spot pressed up against his groin. He closed his eyes on a deep groan, his Adam's apple bobbing again, then he hoisted me back up above dangerous territory.

"Aye, that ye do, lass. That ye do." He shook his head, forcing a serious tone into his voice that I did not want to hear right now. "Tiffany, we can't—"

"Sure, we can." My chest rose and fell against his as my breath grew faster.

His breathing matched mine as he said in a hoarse voice, "But we've had too much to—"

"Honey, I haven't had nearly enough." I cupped his cheeks and stared him in the eyes, letting him see I wasn't even close to being drunk, but I was damn close to exploding in his arms. "I want you," I added seconds before I pressed my lips to his and thrust my tongue inside to do battle with his.

I needed this...I needed him.

He ran one hand up my back to plunge into my hair and cradle my scalp, while the other gripped my bottom hard, pressing me firmly against every blessed inch of him. Tipping my head to the side, he dove his tongue deeper, sweeping every nook and cranny of my mouth, until every pulse in my body vibrated with desire for him.

He set me on the pool table abruptly, finally breaking our kiss as he flattened his palm on my chest and pushed gently until I fell back, my legs still wrapped around him, my dress now hiked to my upper thighs. His gaze devoured me from head to widespread knees, so I slowly inched my dress higher until my barely-there white lace thong peeked out from beneath.

He clenched his jaw, and I could see the muscles bunch as he struggled for control, finally tearing his gaze away from the V of my lacy thong. "We've both had too much to drink, lass. This is probably not a good idea."

"You're right, this isn't a good idea," I said breathlessly, as I undid the buttons on the front of my dress with the built-in bra and peeled the fabric wide, exposing my bare breasts. His pupils dilated, and my nipples hardened as he devoured them with his heated gaze. "This is a great idea." I reached up to cup him through his jeans, and he leaned his head back and let loose a groan that was so deep I felt it clear to my toes.

He focused back on me, looking as though he couldn't take any more, then mumbled something about burning in hell for this as he bent forward at the waist and caught my nipple between his teeth. I squealed as he sucked hard, and I felt the tug all the way to my womb. My eyes rolled back in my head, and I moaned deeply.

There was something about him that drew me to him in a way no other man ever had.

"Ye bewitch me, lass," he mumbled, before taking me in his mouth once again.

"Ditto," I managed, gasping for air.

He was different than any other man I had been with, making me feel alive, making me want him more than I had any man ever, making me need him, and that disturbed me. I liked being in charge, calling the shots. Or maybe it was just the night. The circumstances surrounding the night. The stupid birthday. I didn't know what to think, so I didn't. I just let myself feel.

Because for the first time today, I felt young.

Matt trailed kisses down my stomach through the fabric of my dress, then slid my thong aside and dove his tongue deep. I screamed for all I was worth and plunged my fingers through his blond curly locks, fisting my hands around the silky strands. I couldn't breathe. I wasn't washed up, I wasn't old, I was...beautiful. I cried out as a tidal wave of pure joy consumed me, then the next thing I felt was something massive, stretching me, filling me, and pushing me to the edge of a cliff.

"Yes! God, yes!" This was exactly what I needed, what I longed for, what I wanted with all my soul.

I knew it wouldn't be the same with anyone else. I opened my eyes and met Matt's wide, intense gaze locked solely on me. He knew exactly what he was doing, same as I did, but neither of us was willing to give voice to that. All we were prepared to accept was the fact that we wanted each other, needed each other, more than anything else.

For now, right here in this moment, that was enough.

Matt picked up the pace and I matched his rhythm, until we both were heaving for air and screaming out our release. I dug my fingernails into his arched back, and he gripped my hips, pressing me tighter to him, then he fell forward and collapsed on my chest. I wrapped my arms around him and stroked his back, totally spent. We both just lay there, basking in the pure unadulterated feeling of being completely satiated, even though we were both still nearly fully clothed.

That just made it even sexier.

As the air drifting over us grew cold, Matt stood up and slowly pulled away. I propped myself up on my elbows as a lazy, completely satisfied grin crept over my face, and I met his equally satisfied smile. But then my gaze dropped lower, and my eyes sprang wide at the sheer size of his magnificent penis...but then a realization hit me.

I gasped. "Wait...is that a clover?"

Chapter Three

"The stupid legend? That's what this was about?" Matt yanked up his pants, his face growing rigid. "Yer good, I'll give ye that."

I'd watched in fascination as his shamrock had started to shrink seconds before he'd pulled up his pants, and then his words registered. More precisely, his disgusted tone.

My busted gaze snapped up to his steely one. "Matt, that's not what I meant. I would never—"

"Really, now." He zipped his jeans as I yanked down the hem of my dress and refastened the bodice. "Yer telling me all this," he gestured to the pool table, "wasn't about seeing my so-called tattoo fer yerself?" He crossed his arms over his chest and arched a brow.

"So-called? Honey, I have eyes. I know I saw something." I tried to lighten the tension, because admitting how much I'd needed him was not an option.

He scowled. "Ye don't know what yer talking about.

What ye saw was...ye know what? Never mind. It's not worth it, and ye've pretty much answered me question." Matt shook his head.

"No, I haven't answered your question. What we just did had nothing to do with the legend. Well, maybe originally when the girls..." I started, but Matt looked thoroughly disappointed as he threw up his hands.

He stormed away.

I scrambled off the table and charged after him.

"Matt, wait, it wasn't like that. You made me feel good after a really crappy day. That's what this was about. Just letting ourselves feel good. What's wrong with that?"

"Nothing if that's all ye be looking fer." He turned out the lights as he walked, his back ramrod straight and the set of his shoulders marble stiff. "I just happen to be looking fer something more in a woman, and ye made it perfectly clear yer not on the same page as me. So, what's the point?"

"The point is we connected in a way I never have. I know you felt it," I said from right behind him.

"We connected physically," he stopped abruptly, and I bounced off his back, stumbling a couple steps as he turned around to nail me with a glare, "but that's all there could ever be between us." His gaze ran over me from head to toe, and I felt the chill from four feet away. "Yer not exactly the kind of woman I'd take home to me ma."

I gasped. "Whoever said I wanted to go home to your *ma* anyway?" I narrowed my eyes. "Is this why you stopped popping into my shop? Because I don't meet your standards? Coming from a man who called *me* high maintenance, you have some nerve."

"I'm not the one who's divorced, lass."

I plopped my hands on my hips. "Oh, my God! What are you, a Neanderthal?"

"No, I'm Catholic." He shrugged. "Me family is very old-fashioned. They would never accept me dating a divorced woman."

"Oh, for Pete's sake." I waved one hand in the air.

Matt's family sounded as bad as the people in Mayflower. Because of my grandmother, I had their respect by association, but they'd made it clear they didn't care for my choice of career in teaching sensual massage.

"I'm just being honest with ye, lass," he thrust a finger in my face, "unlike ye were with me."

"Now you're the one who doesn't know what he's talking about." I thrust my finger right back. "And what do you call what we just did, oh saintly one?"

"Based on yer knowledge of me *tattoo*, a poor lapse in judgment." I could see the regret on his face seconds after he said those words, but it was too late.

A sharp pain sliced through me.

I'd been a lot of things in my day, but *never* anyone's 'poor lapse in judgment.' "How will you ever live with yourself now?" I spat. "No wonder you've never been married. A bit strange for a man in his forties who claims to be all about family. Ever think maybe it's not the women? Maybe it's you."

He threw his hands up. "At least I didn't try to trick ye. I was honest. I know what I want."

"I know *exactly* what I want." I grabbed my purse and straightened my dress. "To be as far away from you as I can."

He put his hands on his hips and stared me down. "It's good to know we're finally on the same page, lass."

"My thoughts exactly." I charged past him and headed for the door.

"Tiffany, wait. Let me call you—" Matt started to say from behind me.

"Oh, I think you've called me enough for one night, thank you very much." I swallowed the tears clogging my throat.

His voice gentled. "That's not what I meant."

"Spare me," I managed to get out.

"Look, I can't let you go—"

"You can go to hell," I hollered over my shoulder as the door closed behind me, and I heard him mutter something about *he probably would now*.

He had balls, I'd give him that. Big ones, and I should know.

I charged down the street, too furious to care if anyone saw me coming out of the bar this late at night. A bolt of lightning lit up the black, starless, late May sky, followed by a crack of thunder so loud it shook the ground. I marched on, fearlessly, feeling the same storm raging within me...until a gust of wind carrying the threat of summer and the dewy scent of rain whipped me in the face.

How had this happened?

I hadn't set out to have amazing pool table sex with Matt, it just sort of happened. Two consenting adults had world-rocking physical contact. I sighed, my shoulders relaxing slightly as some of the anger and tension oozed out. He might be acting like an ass now, but I had to admit he'd been upset over me mentioning the clover tattoo. I couldn't blame him, but he wouldn't let me explain.

And then he'd made matters worse by sticking his foot in his mouth several times, insulting my character. If he knew my ex, he would know exactly why I was divorced. Why did the sex with Matt have to be incredible? I'd felt so connected to him, and it had been much more than a physical connection. I wasn't prepared to put a name to what I had felt; but whatever it was, it had been real.

Not up to his standards?

A bit of indignation crept back up my spine, snapping my shoulders straight. Who the hell did he think he was? He was obviously looking for the perfect woman. With today's divorce rate, he wasn't likely to find her. I had news for him. She didn't exist. Not that I wanted to be her. No way in hell. I'd been down that road, and it hadn't been pretty. I liked living my life on my own terms, with no one but myself to think about. I pursed my lips.

Then why was I so angry...so hurt?

Pain pulsed behind my temples from too much thinking and too many martinis. Not to mention getting a little too cozy with my good friend Dom. At the end of the street, I unlocked the door to my shop and was about to march up the stairs to my apartment.

Most of the businesses in Mayflower were set in old houses with apartments upstairs. It cut down on the need for overdevelopment—something this small New England town was dead set against. Suddenly, I felt the presence of someone behind me. I didn't have to turn around to know who followed.

Matt.

I sighed, knowing in my heart he was a good and decent man. He just lived in the stone ages, and I couldn't risk getting hurt any further. I glanced over my shoulder and met his gaze. He stood there larger than life with his hands fisted at his sides, the wind whipping his blond curls about his head like some Viking from long ago, standing strong and proud as he prepared to do battle. Then a solemn expression swept over his face, and the fight went out of him as the first fat raindrops pattered against the hard ground.

We'd both said things we'd never normally say, but we couldn't take them back now. He slipped his hands in his jean pockets and his shoulders drooped slightly, his eyes saying it all. He was sorry. Well, so was I, but that didn't change the fact that we both wanted entirely different things. He was right. What was the point of pursuing something that could lead only to heartache, even if the electricity still sizzled between us?

There *was* no point.

I wasn't ready to share my life, didn't know if I would ever be, and Matt seemed to sense that, which was a good thing. Because had we started something, I didn't know if I would have been strong enough to walk away. I opened the door while I still could, shutting it and him firmly behind me.

I didn't need Matt. I didn't need any man. And so far, turning forty had been eventful, not boring, same as any other age. I took comfort in that. I shook my head and allowed myself a small smile. And here I had been worried.

Silly me for thinking my life was about to change.

"How did this happen?" I whispered one week later, blowing my raw nose and dabbing at eyes that felt like someone had thrown sand in them.

"It will get better, I promise." Zoe squeezed my hand. "Give yourself time."

"Right now, I don't feel like I'll ever get over this kind of heartache." My lips trembled. "Do you realize how different my life will be now?"

"It sucks, I know, Babe." Harmony patted my shoulder from behind me. "But we all saw this coming."

"At least she's at peace now." Morticia stepped up to flank my other side.

"She looks great." I stared down into the plush gold-and-white casket, and fresh tears rolled down my cheeks. "You know how much Grammy's appearance meant to her, and you made her look fabulous. I can't thank you enough for that." I walked down the aisle away from the casket, needing some distance and wanting to give others a chance to pay their respects.

"You're welcome. Dad did a nice job with the calling hours, I thought." Morti and the others followed close by my side.

"The flowers are beautiful. This town really loved Eugenia Eisenhower, that much was evident." Zoe's eyes grew misty. She took a deep breath. "I love this church."

"You're lucky they love you." Harm chuckled. "I still don't think Sister Mary Agnes has recovered from the time your darling daughter used the vibrator she named Snaky to mix the cake batter that you were going to serve at their party. Wonder if they'll ask you to plan this year's Sisters of Sacred Heart Banquette."

My lips tipped up at the corners, remembering our trip to Adult World in Boston. It had been fun shocking Zoe. The best part had been when her cell phone had vibrated next to Katy's Barbie microphone, the whole congregation had gasped, thinking she'd brought Snaky to the Sunday service. I giggled.

That had been priceless.

"Well, it never would have happened if you guys hadn't bought me the ridiculous two-headed monstrosity." Zoe's face paled. "Like I would ever use *that* even when you all thought I needed one, which I didn't by the way."

"She's still in denial." Morti laughed.

"I'm not in denial. I'm the only smart one to know that

thing is just plain freaky." Zoe shuddered. "Besides, now I have Chaz who doesn't need any help in thoroughly satisfying me, thank the Lord."

I actually laughed out loud over that one. "And thank you all for cheering me up." I smiled at each of them. "I don't know what I'd do without any of you, so please don't go MIA on me anytime soon. I can't handle any more change in my life right now."

"Can you handle me?" said a male voice behind me, and my stomach dropped down to my black patent leather toes.

What the hell was *he* doing here?

Inhaling deep, I willed all my anxiety to form in my lungs, and then exhaled the stress on a long slow breath. Thank God for yoga, meditation, and massage. Pasting on a neutral expression, I turned around and looked down my nose at the dark-haired, dark-eyed scum bucket behind me.

Still as handsome as ever, but pure ugliness resided within.

"Bud Grant, what on earth are you doing here?" Thank God for two-inch heels. My ex-husband was only five-foot-eleven when he stood up straight and wasn't trying to fake a bad back. Being six feet with my shoes on put me at least one inch above him.

At this point, I would take any advantage I could get.

"I wouldn't miss this for the world, darling. I am your husband, after all." The corner of his weasel lip hitched up, and I knew he was playing me like he played all women, making me wonder all over again why the hell I had married him in the first place.

"*Ex*," I finally said in disgust. "I certainly pay you enough money each month for you to be a kept man; but trust me, doll, I threw you out five years ago, and I've never been fond of seconds." He was up to something. There was no way he would just randomly show up for Grammy's funeral to pay his respects.

The question was what exactly did he want?

"You've never been fond of siblings, either," my twin sister, Tabatha, said in a sarcastic tone from beside me.

She wore black jeans, sneakers, and a t-shirt. We were identical, but we were nothing alike. I was white diamonds and expensive champagne. She was white gemstones and cheap beer. It wouldn't have mattered one bit to me, but she was the one who had turned up her nose whenever she was in my presence.

I slowly turned to look beyond her, dreading what I knew I would see. Sure enough my biological parents, Charlie and Rita Scott, stood behind Tabatha...the twin they had kept. They claimed they couldn't afford to keep both of us back then, since my mom cleaned houses and my dad was a beer vender.

They'd said it was only temporary, and they would come back for me some day. But once I went to live with my grandmother, they'd never looked back. Grammy had disowned Rita, disapproving of her marriage to Charlie and the fact that they had abandoned their own child. So, I took Grammy's last name and did the same by never looking back.

I'd be damned if I'd start now.

"The only sisters I have are my best friends." Zoe, Morti, and Harm flanked my sides without hesitation, the way I knew they would. "What do you want?"

"We just want to be here for you in your time of need." My mother's tone sounded oddly sincere, as she smoothed her short, golden blonde hair back and lowered her periwinkle blue eyes, so similar to Tabatha's and mine.

I could tell she was nervous, and maybe a little sad, but I didn't let that get to me. She'd had her chance, and I had to stay strong for Grammy. I wrinkled my nose to keep the tears at bay. "Right. Like you've been there for me for the past forty years?"

"Hey, we can't help it your grandmother never let us see you," my father chimed in defensively, giving me a disapproving look for upsetting my mother.

"Oh, don't even go there, Charlie." I refused to call him Dad. "Like you even tried to be a part of my life. You pretty much wrote me off the day she took me in. Can you blame her for writing you three off now?" Grammy had made it clear before she died that they were all cut out of her will.

"They did try. Many times, in fact. You're just too blind to see it." Tabatha looked at me with disgust. "I told you guys this was pointless."

"Tabatha, don't," my mother said softly. "She's been through a lot."

Tabatha threw up her hands. "Like we haven't?" She gave me a look of pure resentment and then stormed off.

A weird feeling swept through my stomach, but I pushed it down. "I don't know what you're talking about. All I know is I never would have made it without Grammy, and I won't let you or anyone else take that away from me."

"I'm so sorry." My mother choked back a sob and then fled the church.

My father stared at me with a frustrated, helpless look. He rubbed his slightly pudgy beer gut, his shoulders slumping in defeat. "I know you don't believe this right now, but I'm sorry, too. All we ever wanted was the best for you, and we've never stopped loving you. From the moment you were born, we knew you were destined for great things. Things only your grandmother could provide."

"That's right." I raised my chin a notch. "She did provide for me, and I owe her everything. Not any of you. I don't owe you a dime."

"And I'm not asking for one. I didn't deserve your mother, and I didn't deserve you. I hope one day you'll come to realize the sacrifice we made and finally learn the truth. We don't care that your Grammy cut us out of her will. We're here for you." And with that, he turned and walked away, looking as though he had the weight of the world on his weary shoulders. His buzzed, balding brown head hung low, and his faded brown eyes stared at the floor.

"Yeah. What they said. I'm here for you, darling," Bud chimed in from beside me, looking anything but sincere.

"You're so fake," I managed to get out. "You make me sick."

He leaned in and didn't bother pretending anymore. "And you're so rich, you make me horny." He grabbed his crotch and leered at me. "You'll be hearing from my lawyer, sweetcakes. With my bad back, I'm thinking you owe me more money every month...now that you're rolling in it."

"And you're a pig." I clenched my fists before I did something stupid and turned around to my friends. "You guys ready to go? I think I've had about enough for one day."

No words were necessary as they hooked my arms and led me out of the church. Just before we walked out the doors, I glanced one last time at my grandmother's casket and tripped over my own feet.

Matt McGinnis stood staring down at Grammy, saying some sort of prayer over her. Then he stepped away but halted when he saw me. He gave me such a sincere look of sympathy and understanding and regret, that I was more tempted than I'd ever been to throw caution to the wind and hurl myself into his arms. One quick glance at my ex reminded me of exactly why I would never do that.

My heart was much more fragile than anyone knew.

Chapter Four

Once again, I was asking myself how this could happen as I sat in my kitchen one week later, waiting for the girls to arrive for our weekly girls' night. We'd taken up comforting each other once a week, rotating houses, like we used to back in our cheerleading days. Only, last week we had missed our meeting because of my grandmother's funeral.

I was sure they were still wondering about the results of our bet on the existence or non-existence of a certain legend tattooed clover, but they had been classy enough not to ask. It had been two weeks since my birthday, and my life was a mess. A complete and utter mess.

I repeat...I hated change, but my life was about to change in a very big way.

The doorbell rang, so I answered. "Hey, girls, come on in."

I stood back and held the door open as Zoe, Harmony,

and Morticia entered. I ushered them into my kitchen and had them sit around my ceramic and glass kitchen table, then I poured them each a drink. A diet cola for Morti, a glass of Chardonnay for Zoe, and a beer for Harm. Normally I opted for a glass of champagne or a martini, but tonight I opened a bottle of sparkling water.

"What was up with your ex showing up?" Morti studied me, looking concerned. "Tell me it's not what I think it is...again."

"He's no fool." The man gave me indigestion. "Now that I have Grammy's inheritance, he's threatening to sue me for more alimony."

"You're shitting me." Harm scowled. "I seriously hate that man."

"He's always been lazy. Even when we were married, he claimed he couldn't work because of a bad back. He was faking it then just like he's faking it now. He can work and support himself just fine. Same with my so-called family only showing up because Grammy cut them out of her will. I'm sure they were *heartbroken* that she didn't leave them anything."

"I don't know. We were there, hon." Zoe gave me a sympathetic look, always the voice of reason. "They sounded really sincere."

"Yeah, I hate to admit it, Tiff, but I agree." Morti shot me an 'I'm sorry' wince.

"What the hell does that mean?" I couldn't believe they were taking anyone's side but mine.

"I can read you like a book, babe. We're not taking

anyone's side. All we're saying is that it might mean there's more to the story than Grammy told you." Harm never held anything back. It was one of the things I liked best about her...not so much at this moment. "I know you might not want to hear this, but they are your only family left. Take it from someone like me. I have a huge family who drive me nuts, but in the end, they are still my family."

"Well, mine has never been there for me." I put some dishes in the dishwasher. "Why should I let them be now?"

"We're not saying you have to accept them. Just be open to listening to what they have to say. What can it hurt?" Zoe jumped up and started helping me.

I just looked at her. "You really have to ask that?"

"None of us want you to get hurt again, Tiff. It's just, you need a support system in your life right now. You're going through so much. I mean, what more can you take, right?" Morti opened another diet cola.

And with that, I burst into tears. "You have no idea."

"Oh, no." Zoe wrapped her arm around my shoulders. "It's not like you to get emotional, Tiff. What's really going on?"

"W-We didn't have a meeting last week, so I couldn't tell you all about that stupid bet." I sniffed, dabbing my eyes.

"Wait...you mean you seriously went through with it?" Harm gaped at me. "I didn't think you were serious."

"It was the night of my birthday." I shrugged. "Call it a moment of weakness. I was feeling insecure."

"You?" Morti's eyebrows shot up.

"I know forty is not old, but I really felt it that night." I smiled fondly. "Matt was there, and he made me feel special. One thing led to another, and well, let's just say there were fireworks after hours."

"Oh, wow, then that means you saw the tattoo." Morti's voice was laced with pure awe and a hint of curiosity.

"I saw something, but I'm not sure what. And that is not why I slept with him at all, but then I made the mistake of revealing that I saw something." I couldn't get the look on his face out of my head. "He was angry and hurt, claiming all I cared about was verifying a stupid legend. I have a feeling many women know about the legend and want to see it for themselves. We both said things we didn't mean, and I left. End of story."

"Not end of story." Harm shook her head hard. "You can't drop that bomb and then not give details."

"And that would make me no better than the other women." I felt terrible for how I must have made Matt feel.

"We're your best friends, not just random people you're telling," Morti said.

"Like I said, I didn't get a good look," I lied.

"Well, there's always next time." Harm wagged her brows.

"Trust me, there won't be a next time." I doubted he would even speak to me again.

"Poor man. He's not a circus animal. If he did get a tattoo there, I bet he's regretting it now." Zoe tsked. "He looks like a god, and with a rumored legend like that, he must attract all sorts of people. No wonder he's single still.

How can he ever trust if a woman truly likes him for who he is and not what he looks like or what tricks he can do."

"He kind of said as much," I admitted. "We're not on the same page. He wants a wife and children. He wants it all, but I don't. I've been down that path, and it wasn't pretty. I'm not going there again. Besides, his family are traditional Catholics who don't believe in divorce, so it's a lose-lose situation. That's why we decided in so many words not to give us a shot."

"Then why the tears?" Harmony glanced at my still wet cheeks and handed me the tissue box.

"Because apparently, it doesn't matter what I want." I started crying all over again and blew my nose.

"What do you mean?" Morti forehead wrinkled. "I'm worried about you, Tiff. You're always so put together. I've never seen you like this."

"Trust me, I'm not put together at all, doll." I half-sobbed, half-hiccupped, taking a sip of water before finally blurting, "I'm late!"

"Oh, hon. No worries there. We'll help you get caught up and back on track with whatever you need." Zoe patted my hand.

"You know how organized I am." I dried my tears to no avail, they just kept coming." I'm not late in *that* way."

"I don't get it." Harm scratched her head.

"How am I going to raise it if I can't even say it." I cried harder.

"Oh, my goodness, you're pregnant." Zoe slapped a hand over her mouth.

I nodded. "I'm on the pill, but I was sick recently, and Matt and I didn't use protection. It was a spontaneous moment of weakness meant to cheer me up on my birthday, nothing more. Or so I thought. My cycle is like clockwork, so I knew something was up when I was late. I took five tests earlier today, and they're all positive. And Matt McGinnis is the father."

They all just stared at me in stunned silence.

"Congratulations?" Harmony said with a questioning tone.

I just shook my head and blew my nose again.

"We're here for you no matter what you decide." Morticia squeezed my hand. "What do you want to do?"

"I don't know." I dried my eyes after the tears finally slowed.

"Are you going to tell Matt?" Morti studied me.

"I'll drop everything and go with you. Just say when." Zoe nodded.

"I appreciate that, but I'm not sure what I'm going to do yet. I know he's the father, but it's my body. I have a lot to think about." My smile was wobbly as I looked around at the women who would do anything for me. "I love you ladies so much. I hope you know that."

They nodded and said it back.

"I'm really tired and need to think. Do you mind if we cut tonight short?"

"Whatever you need, hon. Call us if you need us. You know where we'll be." Zoe hugged me, and they all followed suit before leaving.

What did I want to do...I really had no clue.

THE NEXT MORNING, I still didn't have a clue what I wanted to do. But life went on, and so must I. So, I headed down from my apartment above my massage parlor, Tiffany's Titillating Touch. My house was located at the middle of Lighthouse Lane, across from the park with our town's famous gazebo that held concerts all summer long.

I stepped into the plush waiting room decorated in different shades of relaxing blues, and immediately felt at ease. Sounds of the ocean filtered through the sound system, and a waterfall trickled against the far wall. The lights were on, and the waiting room was full. Trixy had already opened up, thank goodness, while Lucy and Maxim were already giving massages. I used to give massages and was a one-person operation. But now I taught sensual massage, and I had wonderful employees who actually gave the other massages.

"Sorry I'm late," I said to Trixy, my receptionist. "I overslept." That was so unlike me, but I was exhausted.

Trixy wore her bleached blonde hair in pigtails, and it worked for her. She might be young, but she was smart and a whiz with computers. She looked up at me and raised her brows. "Wow, you look...not normal."

My lips parted and my stomach turned over. Could people tell I was pregnant already? "How do you mean?"

"Sorry, I just meant your makeup is usually perfect,

and so is your hair." She chewed her bottom lip. "Don't take this the wrong way, but have you looked in the mirror? One eyebrow is higher than the other, your lipstick is above your lips, and your hair looks like it hasn't been brushed in days." Her gaze dropped to my clothes which were admittedly wrinkled and stained with I didn't want to know what.

"Like I said, I overslept. I was in a hurry."

"Gotcha." She popped her gum, still eyeing me curiously.

"What's the schedule look like for today?" I changed the subject.

"Lucy and Maxim are full, and you had a couples' massage you were going to teach this morning, but they had to rebook. So, you're free if you want to go, um, change, or anything." She shrugged. "Just saying."

What I wanted to do was go back to bed and sleep for a week. I'd taken several more tests and still kept hoping I was wrong. I wasn't. I sighed. "I'm going to take the day off. I have some things I need to take care of."

Trixy nodded then went back to the multiple computer monitors on her desk.

An hour later after a long hot shower, proper hair and makeup, and fresh clothes, I headed outside into the sunshine feeling more like myself than I had during the past two weeks. Glancing a few doors down to McGinny's Pub, I turned in the opposite direction, then headed across the street to the park.

Mayor Edwards stood talking to Officer Donald

Pickles and Fire Chief Wendy Monroe, probably about the Fourth of July party in the park. There would be a parade, food and music in the park, and then fireworks over Freedom Lake.

"Sorry to hear about your grandmother, Ms. Eisenhower." The mayor's voice held genuine sympathy in his tone. He nodded his shiny bald head, his apple cheeks looking more red than usual. "She was a good woman." He ran a hand over his white linen suit that barely stretched over his protruding belly. "My wife, Eleanor, and your grandmother, Eugenia, were good friends. They played Bridge together every week right up until the end."

"Thank you, Mayor Edwards. My grandmother always spoke highly of your Eleanor. Please give her my best."

"Will do." He studied me curiously. "Your grandmother was big on supporting many of Mayflower's causes and events. Can we expect your continued support?" *Since you inherited her fortune?* was implied, but the mayor was a nice man and would never say that out loud.

This town might have loved my grandmother, but they were still on the fence when it came to me. It was no secret my ex-husband was in town, threatening to sue me, and my birth parents and sister had been disowned by my grandmother. I smiled wide. "Of course, I will pick up where my grandmother left off, and maybe add a few causes of my own."

"That's wonderful to hear, my dear. I was hoping we could count on you. My secretary will be in touch after you've had time to sort through your grandmother's affairs." He tipped his head to me.

"I can hardly wait," I mumbled, then waved to Officer Pickles, who blushed, and Fire Chief Monroe, who laughed and waved back.

I turned around to head back across the street toward my house, no longer in the mood for a walk, when I bumped into Matt McGinnis. His hands shot out and he steadied me so I wouldn't fall.

"Whoa, easy there, lass. I wouldn't want ye falling and getting hurt." His gaze ran over me in a non-sexual way as if he were inspecting me for injuries.

He couldn't possibly know, could he?

I cleared my throat, and he dropped his hands. "Thank you. Guess I'd better watch out where I'm going. What are you doing here?"

"Same as ye I suspect." He shrugged, then slid his hands into his jeans' pockets. "Taking a break to stretch my legs. It's a beautiful day."

"It sure is. The days are warming up nicely. It's going to be a good summer. I can feel it." I was saying anything I could to avoid the awkwardness between us.

He hesitated a moment, and then lowered his deep voice an octave. "How are ye doing, lass?"

"I'm fine." I gave my standard answer.

"I mean, really? How are ye coping with losing yer grandmother?" I could hear the sincerity in his tone. He wasn't just asking like most people. He genuinely wanted to know. "I know how much family means to me. I can only imagine the pain ye must feel in losing the woman who raised ye."

My bottom lip wobbled. *Damn hormones.* "It hasn't been easy. She's been such a big part of this town for so long. Everyone loved her. It didn't hurt that she had money, of course. Now everyone wants a piece of me. I don't want to let her down."

"Ye won't. Ye don't owe anyone anything, lass." Eyes so blue and full of warmth and kindness and a little regret stared back at me. "Not even me. I'm sorry fer the way things ended between us."

"Ended? They never began, doll." I winked, sliding into my defense mechanism. Push them away before they could reject me.

"Right." He stared at me for a long moment. "Friends?"

"Friends." I wondered how he would feel if he knew the truth. *If...*because I still wasn't sure what I was going to do.

"Well, as yer friend, I'd better make sure ye get to the other side of the road in one piece." He laughed, distracting me from my thoughts as he looped his arm through mine, and we crossed the street back to our side of Lighthouse Lane.

"Why, thank you, kind sir." I let go of his arm and curtsied with a laugh.

"Yer very welcome, milady." He grinned wide and bowed gallantly at the waist.

"See you around, Matt." I realized we were lingering a

bit too long.

"See ya, Tiff." He saluted me and then headed back to his pub.

The fact that I watched him walk every step of the way didn't go unnoticed by me. I shook off my longing, blaming it on pregnancy hormones. I had to get ahold of myself and fast...before I did something again.

Chapter Five

Two weeks had gone by. I'd been feeling horrible in the mornings and was having a hard time explaining to my staff why I was consistently late for work. I finally made the decision to go to the doctor. Up until now, only my best friends knew about my suspicions and positive pregnancy home tests.

Going to the doctor made it real, and I didn't know if I was ready for that.

I sat in the exam room with Dr. Joy, her black hair cut short and chic. Zoe's fiancé, Dr. Chaz Anderson, also worked there. But since we grew up with him, it felt weird having him as my doctor. The girls had promised not to tell anyone else, including Chaz, until I figured out what to do.

Dr. Joy had given me a urine test as well as an exam and had just come back into the room. She smiled when she made eye contact with me. "Congratulations, Tiffany. You're definitely pregnant. Eight weeks to be exact."

I nodded and sighed. "I guess there's no denying it now."

She looked at me with a blank face. "Is this an unwanted pregnancy?"

"Unplanned, yes. Unwanted...the jury is still out."

"You do have options, you know." One of the things I loved most about Dr. Joy was that she always remained objective and never passed judgement on her client's decisions in a town that was full of judgement.

I nodded. "I know."

"Given your age, this pregnancy will be high risk should you decide to go through with it, but you're in excellent physical condition." She scanned her clipboard. "You'll need to be under the circumstances."

I frowned. "What circumstances? Is there something wrong with me?" My heart rate started speeding up.

"No, no. There's nothing wrong with you, but carrying twins isn't easy for any woman, let alone someone over thirty-five."

I sucked in a sharp breath. "Wait...did you say twins?"

She nodded. "I heard two heartbeats, but I didn't say anything until the ultrasound confirmed it."

I had asked her not to tell me anything until I was ready. My head was spinning. I definitely hadn't been ready for this. I hadn't decided if I wanted one baby, let alone two. But the word *twins* changed everything. I'd spent my life separated from my twin because my parents hadn't been able to afford to raise both of us. Money wouldn't be an issue in this situation, but there was so much else to consider.

The thought that my own parents didn't want me had haunted me my entire life. Thank God for my grandmother who'd always stood by me when even my wayward husband wouldn't. I hadn't been enough for him or my parents or even my sister.

I was spiraling.

Dr. Joy was talking, but the words were just mumbles of sound. She couldn't tell me about all the things I'd missed out on being so alone in the world. But maybe this was a chance to make up for all of that. Maybe this wasn't a crisis, but a blessing.

Maybe.

My grandmother raised me on her own. Yes, there was only one of me, but I was never one to back down from a challenge, and I certainly had the money and the support. How hard could it be?

"So that's pretty much everything for now," Dr. Joy said. "Here's your script for prenatal vitamins, and I'm here if you have any questions."

I realized she'd been talking the entire time I'd been lost in my thoughts. I took the paper from her. "Thanks, Doc."

I left her office and had almost cleared the reception desk when Chaz walked into the lobby. He shook a strand of sandy hair off his forehead, then looked up and noticed me. His hazel eyes brightened, and he smiled wide.

"Tiffany, how are you?" he said with his whisky-smooth voice.

My lower lip wobbled, and I burst into tears. Stupid hormones. Everything was hitting me at once.

His smile slipped. He quickly took my arm and led me toward a chair in the half-full waiting room, felt my hesitation, then steered me down the hall into his office. All sorts of rumors would run rampant within the hour.

"What's the matter?" he asked. "I haven't seen you fall apart like this since I've known you."

I shook my head over and over, still processing the news I'd just received. He handed me a box of tissues, and I blew my nose, then blurted, "I'm pregnant."

He blinked. "I have to admit that's the last thing I expected you to say." He blew out a breath and rubbed his forehead, as if trying to find the right words to say. "Congratulations. Do the girls know?"

"I took several at home tests and told them all, but I made them promise not to say anything until I decided what to do."

"That's fair." He nodded, then said gently, "Do you know what you want to do?"

"I didn't," I replied honestly, "until Dr. Joy just dropped a bomb on me."

"A bomb?" He arched a brow high.

"I'm having twins."

His eyes widened and jaw fell open. "Twins?"

I nodded. "The girls don't even know that one yet. I'm still processing everything. All I know is whether I planned this or not, I will never make my children feel what I felt when my parents gave me up."

"Okay, well, you know you have a big support system here. Your friends love you. We all do." He cleared his throat. "Is the father in the picture?"

I hesitated, then finally admitted, "The father is Matt McGinnis." It felt good to tell my secret out loud. Freeing somehow. "I haven't told him yet because I wasn't sure what I was going to do. But now that I'm keeping the babies, he has a right to know he's going to be a father."

Chaz nodded. "Matt's a great guy. I'm sure he'll step up and do the right thing."

"I don't want him to do anything. I just want him to know. If he wants to be in their lives, I would never deny him that. But I don't need any help providing for my family."

"We're talking about a proud Irishman here." Chaz chuckled. "Good luck with that one." He stood. "I've got to get back to my patients. Are you okay to leave on your own? Should I call Zoe to take you home?"

I shook my head. "No, I'm good. Thanks, Chaz. You really helped." I stood and picked up my purse. "I'm not going home. I'm going to see a proud Irishman." I held my head high and took the first step towards my new life.

IT WAS LUNCHTIME, and I was starving. I'd been having morning sickness that was awful, but by lunch, I more than made up for it. McGinny's Pub was packed as usual. Great atmosphere, great music, great food, great hospitality...

What more could anyone want?

The hostess seated me at a table in the bar, and I ordered enough food for three people. Then I waited for Matt to make eye contact with me. He finally did, and I motioned for him to come over. He gave me a nod, then said something to the bartender before slinging a cloth over his shoulder and heading my way.

"What'll it be, lass? A martini? Champagne?" He grinned as he reached my table. A big, strapping, dirty-blond, curly-haired Irishman. He was so tall and ruggedly handsome I had to remind myself we were just friends.

I tore my gaze away from his bulging muscles and tossed my long, golden-blonde curls over my shoulder. "It's a bit early for that."

He shrugged. "It's five o'clock somewhere. Besides, lots of people have a drink on their lunch break."

"True, but I'm not much of a drinker these days. I already placed my lunch order, but I'll have some water, please."

He nodded once then walked away to pour me a glass of ice water himself, not above serving his customers even though he owned the place. He carried it back to me and set it on the table then looked around. "Ye here alone?"

I nodded, taking a big drink as I gathered the courage to say what had to be said. "Do you have a minute to sit? I wanted to talk to you about something."

He eyed me curiously as he sat. "I always have time fer

a friend." He watched me as if testing his words to see if that term still applied.

"Good." I smiled slightly, trying to reassure him, but I felt like it was more of a grimace. My heartbeat sped up, and I suddenly felt warm. I fanned my face.

"Are ye alright, lass? Ye look flushed."

The waitress came out and set all my entrees on the table in front of me. Matt's eyebrows shot up to his hairline.

"I'm fine. Just a little lightheaded. Low blood sugar and all that." I grabbed a turkey sandwich and took a big bite.

"I see." He chuckled. "I like a woman who knows how to eat."

"Then you're gonna love me." I dug into my soup.

He leaned back and folded his arms, watching me in awe as I shoved a heaping spoonful of macaroni and cheese into my mouth next.

"Sorry," I managed to get out. "Hungry."

"By all means eat first. We can talk after. I wouldn't want yer food to get cold." He watched me, waiting patiently as I worked my way through all three entrees plus dessert. No need for a doggie bag for me. "I've been having some stomach issues lately, so when I finally feel good, I take advantage of it and eat my fill."

"Nothing wrong with that." His eyes softened. "I have to say I'm glad to see ye again. I know ye said we could be friends, but I haven't seen ye around town at all over the past two weeks. I thought maybe ye'd changed yer mind."

"No, I still want to be friends." I wiped my mouth with a napkin. "I, um, just had some thinking to do."

"I'm sure yer still grieving yer grandmother's passing. That has to be difficult." His voice filled with sympathy. "I'm here if ye need to talk, lass."

My heart warmed. "I appreciate that." Then my jaw hardened. "I'm also dealing with my ex-husband. He found out my grandmother left everything to me, so now he's threatening to sue me for more alimony."

Matt's deep dimples disappeared as his smile slipped. "He sounds like a real piece of work."

"You have no idea. And there's also my parents and sister who insist on hanging around town until I hear them out." I knew they lived close, but I'd never seen them around as much as I had lately.

He studied me with his penetrating blue eyes. "I take it ye don't want to do that."

"I don't know what I want." I shook my head, forcing my mixed emotions down so they wouldn't consume me.

"That's fair." He nodded. "Having family come back into yer life is a big change. I know family isn't always easy, but they are still yer flesh and blood. Maybe just keep an open mind, lass. Hear what they have to say. What can it hurt?"

Plenty, I thought.

I'd been hurt enough by my family for one lifetime, thank you very much. I wasn't ready to deal with any of them. "I don't do well with change." I took a deep breath.

"My life has changed in a lot of ways since my fortieth birthday."

"It sounds it." He shrugged. "Change doesn't have to be bad; ye know. It can be a good thing, too."

"I, um, I'm glad to hear you say that because I am not the only one who's life is about to change."

His brow puckered. "What do ye mean?"

"You said that family means a lot to you, right?" I watched his expression go from confused to beaming.

"Absolutely. Family is everything."

"Right. And one day you want a family of your own, correct?" I bit my bottom lip, keeping my eyes locked onto his.

His expression grew guarded. Suspicious. "Yes, but ye made it clear that ye didn't want marriage or a family. Did ye meet someone else?"

I was already shaking my head. "No, it's nothing like that."

"Then what could have changed that has to do with me?"

I couldn't take it anymore, so I blurted, "I'm pregnant."

He blinked and sat there for a full stunned minute. "Are ye saying I'm going to be a father?"

I nodded slowly, relieved he didn't question *if* he was the father. Because that would imply that I slept around. I might be a modern woman, but I still only slept with one man at a time.

I cleared my throat. "Yes."

He rubbed his jaw. "From our one night in the Pub?"

I nodded again. "There's more."

"More? What more could there possibly be?"

"We're having twins."

His jaw fell open and the rag slung over his shoulder fell to the table. He gaped at me and scrubbed a hand over his smooth-shaven jaw. "Are ye sure?"

"Dr. Joy confirmed it just this morning." I still couldn't believe I was responsible for growing one human being, let alone two. Then I had to raise them and try not to make a train wreck of their lives. "I'm eight weeks now."

"Twins...." he breathed the words out, sounding more in awe this time rather than in shock. He slapped a hand down on the table and grabbed the rag then slung it back over his massive shoulder. "Well, that settles it, then."

This time I frowned as an uneasy feeling filled me. "Settles what?"

"We're getting married." He gave me a wide-toothed grin.

"E-Excuse me?" I sputtered.

"Ye heard me, lass. I'll call me mum and make all the arrangements. Ye won't have to do a thing." His accent thickened with his excitement.

"But you said they won't accept me," I managed to get out, as my own level of shock set in. This conversation had taken a turn I wasn't prepared for.

"I was just mad at ye because ye used me over a stupid bet, when I really liked ye. Besides, ye said ye didn't want marriage or children, and I did, so what was the point of starting something? Me mammy will be thrilled to be a grandmammy." He beamed. "As thrilled as I am to be a daddy."

I threw up my hands. "You've lost your mind, Matthew McGinnis."

He hoisted a shoulder. "Can't a fella do the right thing?"

I was already shaking my head. "Give me some credit. I would never get married just because I'm pregnant."

He rubbed a hand over his smooth-shaven jaw. "Then why did ye tell me?"

"Because *I* was trying to do the right thing." I tossed down money on the bill. "I am perfectly capable of taking care of myself and my children."

He threw my money back at me. "Yer money is no good here from now on. And I plan to take care of *me* children, too."

"I would never deny them their father," I said carefully to be sure he understood me, "but that doesn't mean I need your help."

"Ye may not think ye don't, but mark me words, yer going to get it." He thrust a finger in my direction as he stood up. "A McGinnis never breaks his word." Then the stubborn man stormed back over behind the bar.

I could be stubborn too. I blew out a frustrated breath...

What the hell had I gotten myself into?

Chapter Six

The next day I met old man Truman Winters at my mailbox out front on Lighthouse Lane. Truman was nearly blind and a bit forgetful. Even with his coke-bottle glasses, he still delivered the wrong mail to people on a daily basis. He really should retire, but he was the nicest man in town, and being Mayflower's mail carrier gave him a purpose since his wife passed away years ago.

Zoe hooked him up with pies each week, Harm gave him a different essential oil each week, Morti had coffee talks weekly, and I had my staff give him a therapeutic massage monthly. He was a special man to us all.

"Good morning, Ms. Eisenhower." Truman tipped his head gallantly, his mailbag slung across his body and over his shoulder."

"Good morning, Truman." I smiled wide. "How's the back?"

"Right as rain, I supposed, though I don't know how

right rain is. All I know is it's going to rain soon. My knees are telling me so something fierce."

I looked at the cloudless sky, but past experience told me Truman knew best when it came to the weather. "Glad to hear that massage is helping. Come back any time. We'll get those knees fixed."

"You girls are so good to me." He shook his gray head and pushed his thick glasses up his nose. "Don't know what I did to deserve all the love."

"Look at you." I winked. "What's not to love?"

He blushed. "Speaking of love, I hear congratulations are in order for you and Mr. McGinnis. Twins! Isn't that somethin'?"

The rumor mill in Mayflower was about as rampant as they came. I should have known everyone would know by now, especially since Gerty and Gabby Rogers had been at the doctor's the same day as me. Nothing got by those two.

"It sure is something." I smiled through clenched teeth.

"Best of luck to you both. Babies are a miracle if you're lucky enough to be blessed with them." His eyes grew misty. He and his late wife had never conceived. This town was all he had left. "Oh, before I forget, I got a package for you today."

I took the padded envelope from him and discreetly checked the name to be sure it belonged to me. It did, so I smiled. "Thank you, Truman. You have a good day... despite the rain." I glanced at the still cloudless sky.

"Gonna be a doozy," he said, and hurried on his way

just as a rumble of thunder sounded way off in the distance.

I just shook my head and opened my package as I walked back toward my front door. And stopped. And stared. I sat down on a chair on the front porch of my building. A scarlet letter, only this one was an H instead of an A. The word Harlot was written across a single piece of paper. No signature. Cowards.

I wasn't an adulteress or a harlot. I was simply an unwed mother.

This town was so old-fashioned. Most likely Gerty and Gabby—the town's resident busybody troublemakers—had heard that Matt had proposed, and I said no. If you could even call it a proposal. It had been more like an order. Nothing romantic about it. This wasn't the seventeenth century, for crying out loud. I wasn't going to marry a man who didn't even love me.

I wasn't going to marry a man, period.

End of story.

Amen.

All I wanted was the same respect they had shown my grandmother. Was that too much to ask? Apparently so, yet they expected me to continue supporting her causes with my inheritance. I sighed, feeling emotional. I wasn't a weepy kind of woman, but ever since my diagnosis, I felt on the verge of tears constantly.

Diagnosis.

I chuckled inwardly. A diagnosis implied there was something wrong with me. Babies weren't a disease, but pregnancy was a condition. And being pregnant with twins at forty was a high-risk condition at that. Chocolate. Maybe that was what I needed. I stood and was about to enter my house when I saw Bitsy Beaumont walking down the street.

Bitsy was a party planner, but she was more the traditional kind, which this town was all about. Not long ago she and Zoe had been competing to win the bid to plan the Labor Day Bash for the mayor, and he had been looking for something fresh and new. Zoe had turned her catering business into a full-blown modern party-planning business, winning the bid.

Bitsy left town shortly after. She normally looked so put together, like Martha Stewart, but the competition had taken its toll on her. She'd left town looking frazzled. We all had assumed she needed a break from Mayflower and had taken her business somewhere else to start over.

I studied her closer...

Bitsy Beaumont was pregnant!

But why were people stopping her, smiling, and acting like she was the town's pride and joy? No scarlet letter for her. Meanwhile, the old gossips crossed the street when they saw me coming.

Principal Brimstone came out of a bakery and handed Bitsy a pastry and a glass of milk, then slid his arm around her as they walked my way. As they drew closer, I saw the last of the sunlight shine off the massive ring on her finger, and realization dawned.

Bitsy had said *yes*.

A flash of what my life might have looked like had I said *yes* to Matt was right in front of me. I could have had it all: a man to call my own, a family that was mine...respect. Instead, I was the town harlot, while she was the not-so-virgin Mary.

I turned toward the door to my salon, intending to raid my chocolate stash and eat it all in one sitting. Even if I had heartburn for days, it would be worth it. I reached for the doorknob when a voice rang out behind me.

"Tiffany Eisenhower, how nice to see you again," the feminine voice purred.

I pasted on a smile and slowly turned around. "Bitsy Beaumont, what a surprise."

"It's Brimstone now. Bitsy Brimstone, right, darling?" She smiled up at the man beside her, running a hand over her rounded stomach. I didn't know anything about babies, but if I was two months along, she had to be four or five.

His face flushed bright red, the thin strands of black hair combed over his bald spot slipping as he cleared his throat. Pulling at the collar of his shirt, he replied, "Uh... right, darling."

"Congratulations to the both of you," I said.

"Thank you. Isn't it a miracle?" Bitsy shook her head in wonder. "I didn't think I could have children."

"Neither did I," Brimstone muttered.

Bitsy went on as if she hadn't heard him. "This town has welcomed me back with open arms, all because my Roger made an honest woman out of me."

"Yes, well, a man of honor does the right thing." He had the nerve to look down his nose at me. "Or *tries* to."

"Well, I for one, don't care to be in a loveless marriage just because I'm pregnant." I looked at Bitsy, but my comment went completely over her head.

Brimstone narrowed his eyes, reading me loud and clear.

"Come along, darling." He guided Bitsy across the street, talking as he walked. "We need to get you and the baby out of the elements." He glanced back at me. "A storm's coming, and I don't want to be anywhere near it when it hits."

A rumble of thunder sounded closer this time, and they picked up the pace until they disappeared down the street. The first fat raindrops began to fall, and I hurried inside my house to my apartment upstairs, feeling more alone than ever.

A COUPLE HOURS LATER, a knock sounded on my door.

I frowned and looked through the peephole, then burst into tears as I gladly opened the door. Zoe quickly stepped inside, carrying the casserole she'd made me to my kitchen counter, and then giving me a big hug.

"What is wrong with me?" I asked. "All I do is cry... and throw up...and eat." I inhaled the smell of chicken, cheese, stuffing, and seasonings, my mouth watering instantly.

"It's called the first trimester, hon." She patted my back before letting me go. "It'll get better. I promise."

I grabbed a couple of plates from my cupboards and some silverware from the drawer. "Thank you for dinner. I know how busy you are with running four kids around, organizing the Labor Day Bash, and planning your wedding."

"True, but it's finally summer. School's out, so we don't have nearly as many extracurricular activities going on. Not to mention, I'm not alone in this anymore. I have Chaz." She smiled gently and declined the plate I tried to hand her. "I already ate, but I'll sit with you while you eat. You don't have to be alone, either, you know."

"I am never getting married again." I shoved a forkful of food into my mouth, still amazed at how hungry I could be after being so sick in the morning.

"I'm not talking marriage necessarily. Just letting someone help you. The girls and I heard about Matt's proposal."

"I was just about to text you all before you came over. It's been a day. That's for sure." I refilled my plate and headed to the living room.

Zoe grabbed two bottles of water and followed me. "It sounds it. Twins? That's incredible, Tiff." She handed me one bottle as she curled up on the couch.

"Thanks, doll." I took the bottle from her and drank deeply. I thought about her words. "It *is* incredible and terrifying!"

"You're a rockstar. You can do anything." Zoe studied

me. "I take it your talk went well with Matt if he proposed. How romantic."

"He didn't ask me to marry him." I blew out a big breath. "He stated we would get married as if it were a fact. Nothing romantic about it."

"And you said no," she said softly.

"Of course, I said *no*. I have my own money. I don't need his. I'm all for him having rights and being a part of his children's lives, but that doesn't require me marrying another man who doesn't even love me."

"How do you know he doesn't?"

I looked her in the eyes. "Because he barely even knows me." I thought about that. Did he have an ulterior motive? "There has to be another reason he's so adamant about marrying me." I didn't trust men after all the men in my life had let me down.

"Um, you're having his babies." She grinned wide and chuckled. "I think he knows you quite well."

I rolled my eyes and laughed, then sobered. "He knows me physically, but he has no clue what kind of person I am. He judged me because of my divorce, slept with me anyway, and now he wants to do the right thing by marrying me. I'll pass, thank you very much."

"I don't blame you, but I hope you know you have us." She rubbed her hands together. "We're going to be the best aunties to your beautiful babies. They are going to be gorgeous with you and Matt as the parents."

"Well, there is that." I laughed, trying to see the bright

side to my situation. "Seriously, though. I am grateful to have you girls in my life."

"Always." She squeezed my hand. "So, what's next?"

"I don't have a clue. I was hoping you would tell me." I was in way over my head when it came to babies.

"We go shopping for maternity clothes." Zoe nodded.

My eyes widened with a very real understanding of what was to come. "Oh, no, you mean I actually have to wear the dreaded granny panties?"

"Hey, my undergarments are not granny panties. At least not now. And no, you'll be wearing maternity panties."

I groaned. "I don't see much difference."

"Hey, trust me, when you get in your last trimester, you'll appreciate having comfy clothes."

"Oh, and don't bother throwing me a baby shower. I'm wealthy and old enough to buy my own things. Besides, no one would come except you girls and my employees. I don't need that kind of hit to my self-esteem."

"The town will come around. Look at how they were after Max left me. I thought they would never see me as anything except the ex-fire chief's wife. No one took me or my business seriously until I won the Labor Day Bash."

"All I know is they loved my grandmother, and I am most definitely not her." She was fierce and independent like me, yet traditional like the town.

"They loved her because she spent her money on Mayflower. You'll figure out what's important to you and do the same."

"That's just it. They didn't ask me if I wanted to do the same, they just expected me to. That's the frustrating part. I had already planned to keep Grammy's investments going because they were important to her, but the least they could do is treat me with respect."

"How have they disrespected you? Did something happen?"

I walked over to my desk and pulled out a piece of paper. "I got this in the mail today." I showed her the red H.

Zoe gasped. "Who sent that?"

I shrugged. "There was no name or return address. I have a hunch it was the Rogers sisters."

"Well, that would explain it. Remember the petition they organized for a lower curfew because of the scandal surrounding Lexi?" Zoe's daughter had been accused of spreading indecent pictures of herself around, but the rumors weren't true.

"Yes, but the truth came out in the end, thank goodness, and the curfew didn't stick."

"True, but it wouldn't surprise me if those old biddy hypochondriacs were up to their crazy antics again. That's just so wrong. Not to mention unfair and not true. They shouldn't get away with it." Zoe shook her head. "What are you going to do?"

That seemed to be the question of my life lately. "Beat them at their own game." I stared at the envelope on the table. "I have an idea. My Grammy always said, *when life hands you lemons, make lemonade*...with a splash of gin, of course." I shrugged. "I just have to find my gin."

75

Chapter Seven

The Fourth of July dawned sunny with the promise of a warm day. I taught a sensual massage session to a young couple in the morning, and then I headed to the park in the afternoon for the day's festivities. There was a parade in the morning that ended in the park, followed by food trucks and live music. Half the town had closed shop early because Mayflower took their festivals seriously.

The fireworks would take place over Freedom Lake after it got dark. Harmony and Morticia waved, saving me a spot on a blanket in front of the gazebo. On a blanket next to them were Zoe, her children, and Chaz. I waved and made my way through the crowd until I reached them.

"I'm so hungry." I sat on a blanket. "I'm seriously always so hungry."

"Get used to it, babe." Harmony chuckled. "Have you seen the size of your babies' father?"

My gaze slid over to Matt, who was running his food

truck while his cousin sang Irish music on the stage in the gazebo. As if drawn to me, Matt made eye contact and smiled wide as he waved. I swallowed hard, trying not to notice how big his biceps were. How big his entire body was. I waved back then looked away.

"I still can't believe you're having twins." Morticia stared at my stomach in wonder. "The human body is miraculous. I mean, even with all your organs, it still finds room for two babies. Two! That's insane." Her eyes met my terrified ones, and her smile slipped. "Sorry. Didn't mean to freak you out." She bit her bottom lip.

"You're not telling me anything I haven't already thought about. How am I supposed to deliver two bear cubs?" I grumbled. "They're literally going to be huge because of him. It's all his fault. Everything is his fault." I knew that wasn't true, but I needed someone to blame for my stupidity in not using protection. We weren't teenagers.

How could we both have been so foolish?

I had only cared that I was on the pill at the time, but obviously that hadn't worked for me. I never gave a second thought as to why I should still use protection beyond the pregnancy risk. Matt didn't seem like the kind of guy who slept around, but even I knew, it only took once of sleeping with the wrong person to contract a disease. I'd since then been tested, and I was clean, thank goodness. Still, I hadn't been that reckless ever. It just proved how hard I had taken turning forty.

And now I was paying the consequences.

"Interesting brooch." Zoe joined us on our blanket. "I see you found your gin." She winked.

"Gin?" Morti looked back and forth between the two of us.

I touched the red ruby H gemstone with the solid gold cape draped behind it. "I sure did. I took the insulting design my secret admirer sent me and gave it to my jeweler to make into something complementary." I winked. "She custom created this for me and put a rush on it. Don't you just love it?"

"Secret admirer?" Harm raised both her eyebrows and also looked between Zoe and me. "What's going on?"

"I think she means whoever sent her the red H for harlot," Zoe clarified, adding, "but I don't think it's much of a secret."

"Oh, yeah, duh." Harm slapped her forehead.

Gerty and Gabby Rogers walked by at that moment and gaped at my chest, their jaws falling open as they stared at my brooch. Giving me a dirty look, they stuck their noses in the air and hurried their way over to Sister Mary Agnes and Father O'Dority.

I could only imagine the earful they were giving them.

I waved.

"I just love you." Harm grinned while shaking her head. "You don't care what anyone thinks, Tiff."

"Actually, I do." I sighed. "More so as I get older. And being pregnant is making it worse than ever. I feel like I'm on the verge of tears all the time or I'm laughing hysterically at nothing. I feel like a crazy person."

"Pregnancy hormones are no joke," Zoe said.

"Want some food?" Morticia asked. "I thought you said you were hungry."

"I was, but I suddenly lost my appetite." I had no sooner said the words than I saw Matthew McGinnis headed my way with a heaping plate in his hands.

"Well, isn't that just the sweetest thing." Zoe clapped.

"The sweetest." I tried not to grind my teeth.

I had told him I wanted him to be there for his children, not for me. He was already trying to take care of me. Why? The twins weren't even born yet. What did he want from me? He definitely must have an ulterior motive.

"Ladies, Chaz, kids." Matt nodded his head once at each of them, his dimples sinking deep as he smiled when his eyes locked on mine. "Tiffany," he said, his voice making my name sound like a caress. He looked more handsome than a man had a right to as he leaned over and tried to hand me a heaping plate of food. "I thought ye might be hungry, and I haven't seen ye eat anything since ye got here."

"Thanks, but I'm not really hungry." My stomach rumbled loudly.

He arched a shaggy blond brow high. "Really. Me wee babes must be talking already then." He winked.

I rolled my eyes. "I can take care of myself, remember?"

He narrowed his. "And I plan to help take care of me babies, *remember?*"

I gestured to the plate he still held in his big hands.

"So, you're saying that plate of food is for them and not me?"

He shrugged his massive shoulders. "Whatever it takes to make ye eat it, lass, then yes. None of the food is fer ye."

I sighed in dramatic fashion. "Fine, for the sake of your wee babes." I took the plate from him and dug in with more gusto than I had intended to show.

He laughed. "Nice brooch. What's it stand fer?"

"Hero," I raised my chin a notch, "because I am the hero of my own story."

"I like that." He nodded. "Well, I'd better get back before me cousin burns McGinny's food truck down."

I puckered my forehead and looked at the stage. "I thought your cousin was the singer over there."

"He is. That would be Finn. He sings at McGinny's Pub as well. My other cousin, Aidan, is helping with the food, though I don't know if that's a good idea or not. That lad hasn't quite figured out his path in life yet."

Have any of us?

Matt chuckled. "Let's just say there are a lot of us."

"Lucky you," I said and meant it. I'd only had my grandmother, but since her death, I felt like I didn't have anyone. The girls were an exception, but they weren't blood.

"Lucky fer our babes, too." He tilted his head in salute and then headed back to his food truck.

I thought about what he said. Our children would be very lucky indeed to have a big family like Matt's in their lives. They would never have to feel alone or unloved or unwanted...ever!

Swallowing the lump in my throat, I needed a moment alone. I got up and walked over to the nearest trash can to throw my empty plate away. Empty? I blinked, just realizing I'd finished it all.

"Hi, Tiffany," a soft voice came from behind me.

I inhaled a deep breath then turned around to face my birth mother. "Rita." I looked behind her but didn't see anyone. "I'm surprised to see you here alone. Where are Charlie and Tabatha?"

"Oh, they're over in front of the gazebo. That Finn McGinnis is so talented. He'll melt your heart with one song." Her face brightened.

"So, I've heard." I studied her. "What do you want from me, Rita?"

Her face fell. "What do I want from you?" She paused a beat, and I could see her throat working. "Everything," she finally got out. "What do I expect from you?" She shook her head. "Nothing." She nodded as if resigned to her fate. "What do I hope you will give me?" She looked me in the eye with sincerity even I couldn't deny. "A chance to get to know you."

I hesitated a moment. "You don't want my money?"

Her face pinched with pain, and she shook her head hard. "If I had wanted money, I never would have defied my mother and married your father for love."

"Love?" A sob slipped out. "You gave me away. Who does that?"

"It wasn't like that," her voice softened, "it was never supposed to be like that."

"I don't understand."

"I know you don't, but maybe it's time that you did."

"What are you saying?"

She shrugged, kicking the dirt ground with a worn, dusty sneaker before leveling her gaze back on me. "I heard you were pregnant with twins. Congratulations."

I fought the urge to laugh at the irony of it all. "That's rich. Kind regards for a woman who clearly didn't feel the same way about her babies."

"I probably deserve that," she conceded. "But you don't know all of it."

It was true that I didn't, but there was a part of me not that interested in hearing about it anyway. "Ever hear of too little, too late, Rita?"

"It's never going to be the right time or place."

"You're right. Say your piece and get it over with."

"My mother made me choose between her and your father. There was never any choice. I loved your father with all my heart. So, when I chose him, she cut me off. We would have been fine, but we got pregnant with twins. There was no way we could afford to care for both of you at the same time. I went to my mother for help. She took one look at you and somehow knew you were more like her than me. She made a deal with me. Let her care for you until we got on our feet, and then she would give you back to us."

"Wait...Grammy made the deal?" My heart squeezed

tight, and I felt like I couldn't breathe. "I-I thought you did."

"No, *she* made the deal...but I did say yes. I had no choice, but I honestly thought she would keep her end of the agreement." Rita looked me in the eye with such despair and regret. "When I went back for you, she refused to give you back to me. She didn't want the rest of us. You were the daughter she always wanted but never had. So, she shut me and her other granddaughter—your sister—out."

I was already shaking my head. It couldn't be true. The grandmother who was a mother to me couldn't have kept me from my own mother...could she? I swallowed the lump in my throat. "I don't believe you."

"I understand why you don't, but it's true. The woman you knew was a far different person than the woman I knew. I was weak in her eyes. You weren't." Rita's voice cracked. "We never would have agreed to the deal if we had known it would mean losing you. I just hope we haven't lost you forever."

I wiped away the tears now streaming down my face. "Why didn't you fight harder for me?"

"She was too powerful. What could I do? I spent years trying to get her to change her mind and let me at least see you. Instead, she spent her life turning you against me."

"This is too much. I can't handle it. I guess you know everything." I huffed out a breath and crossed my arms over my chest.

"I don't know everything," she said quietly, "but I do

know a thing or two about carrying twins. I'd like to be a part of your life if you'll let me. This might be my only chance to be a grandmother."

I frowned. "What about Tabatha?"

Rita was already shaking her head. "She married young, right out of college, but her husband and daughter died when their house caught fire. They didn't have a lot, but they were happy. Everything was destroyed. She never moved on and hasn't been the same since. That's why she's so bitter and angry. You're just her scapegoat, unfortunately."

"I didn't know," I said softly. "When did that happen?"

"Fifteen years ago." Rita shrugged. "She kept it pretty quiet. Your grandmother didn't even know she'd married and had a child. Tabatha was hurt and angry at her for never wanting anything to do with her, only you. She didn't want to share her own daughter, and after the tragedy, she didn't want your grandmother's pity."

I was twenty-five and single then. I remembered having dreams of burning up in a fire. I would wake up sweating, feeling like I couldn't breathe for months. It took months of therapy to get past that. I had no idea it could be a twin connection. My heart ached over the thought of what Tabatha must have gone through. Was still apparently going through.

"So, she's all alone now?" I asked quietly.

Rita looked sad as she nodded. "At least she has us."

I felt my brow pucker. "What about friends?"

"They had friends as a couple, but she avoided them

until they gave up and stopped trying. She couldn't handle any reminders of what she'd lost. Her job is pretty isolating, so it's hard for her to meet people. She's an artist, and a talented one at that. An illustrator for children's books, but she works remotely. Her work has taken off, and she does well for herself now. She lives in a small apartment, and that works for her."

"Well, I feel bad for her, but I don't know what you want me to do about it?"

Rita stared at me for a long moment. "Not everyone wants something from you, Tiffany. Maybe we just want to be there for you with nothing in return."

I shrugged. "Forgive me if I'm having a hard time believing that. People have always wanted something from me for my entire life."

"Well, maybe it's time that changed. Just think about it, okay?"

I slowly nodded. "Okay."

"I'd better get back before your father starts to worry about me." She walked away before I could tell her *no*.

For the first time in a long time...I wasn't sure I wanted to.

Chapter Eight

I pulled into the three-lane driveway of Chaz's—and now Zoe's—enormous Victorian house with the wrap-around porch on Hope Lane. It had to be five thousand square feet. Soft almond siding with hunter Hunter green shutters decorated the outside, and the mansion sat on a lot twice the size of any other house on the block. It reminded me of my grandmother's house before she sold it and moved into a condo on the lake, after I grew up and moved out.

The Andersons had clout.

Looked like the zoning board had made more than a few allowances. It didn't hurt that his parents were former members of the board, current members of the historical society and town council, and his father had even been mayor years ago. They had retired to Florida but still spent half the year in Mayflower. Zoe had the town wrapped around her finger as their favorite party planner, not to mention she was engaged to their beloved doctor.

Meanwhile, I was still the pregnant harlot with the risqué job who'd said *no*.

I sighed as I parked my car and headed inside. It looked like Harm and Morti were already here. All the kids were at sleepovers, and Chaz was at the pub with Matt. They had become pretty good friends since he'd gone to Chaz for help in processing the idea of becoming a father and learning what he could do to help.

The kitchen consisted of tons of counter space, tiled backdrop, quartz countertops, and an enormous island with a flattop range built right in. A large black iron wagon wheel hung above it, with cast iron pots and pans dangling. A second oven and microwave were built into the wall beside the cabinets, right next to the wine bar and break-fast nook. There was a formal dining room as well, but we preferred to sit at the island.

"So glad you're up to girls' night, Tiff." Zoe handed me a glass of sparkling water. "I wasn't sure, with how you've been feeling."

"Nothing can keep me away from your cooking." I took a big sip of the water as I sat on a barstool.

Glancing around and inhaling the delicious aroma, I tried not to drool over the display before me. She'd gone all out as usual, cooking up a storm. French cuisine this time, my favorite. She had French Onion Soup to start, then Coq au vin, followed by crème brulée.

"How far along are you now?" Harm glanced at my

stomach and took a sip of her beer followed by a bite of cheese.

"Ten weeks." I nibbled on a cracker.

"You're not even showing yet." Morti studied me.

"The morning sickness will go away at the end of the first trimester, around twelve weeks. Usually for a first baby you won't show until around sixteen weeks, but for twins you'll probably notice a difference at twelve weeks." Zoe winked.

"Great, only two more weeks until I have to start wearing maternity clothes." I sighed, so not looking forward to that.

"The clothes today have come a long way. You should have seen the ugly outfits I wore when I was pregnant with Lexi sixteen years ago. I wore the same for Troy thirteen years ago, but thank goodness, I got new ones for Bobby six years ago, and even newer ones for Katy three years ago. I would pass them on, but trust me, you won't want them. Not to mention, I have curves, while you look like a fitness model."

"Not for long at this rate," I muttered, feeling uncomfortable in my own skin. A first for me. "I'm sick of talking about me. What's going on with you all?"

"Well, planning the Labor Day Bash is stressful enough. I don't want to let the mayor down since he believed in me enough to choose me to plan this big event. And now Bitsy's back and already married." Zoe took a sip of her chardonnay. "On top of that, my mother and former mother-in-law are pushing me to start wedding planning."

"I love Wilma and Lilabelle." I grinned, thinking of them and their crazy antics. "At least you know they care." I thought of my own family who *said* they cared, but I couldn't even fathom that my grandmother had lied to me. She had been my everything.

If it was true, why hadn't she told me?

"I wish they didn't care quite so much. Thank goodness Chaz's mother, Roz, isn't interfering."

"Yet." I scoffed.

My ex-husband's mother had been a nightmare when we got married. That should have been my first red flag. She hadn't liked me then and liked me even less now. She had tried to take over and make the wedding hers because I had taken away her baby boy. I'd gladly given him back after our divorce, but he hadn't moved on without me.

I'd always been a sucker for pretty things. He was still gorgeous, but no other woman was dumb enough to support his sorry ass. Mommy Dearest was tickled pink to have him to herself, which was yet another thing Bud hated me for.

His mother drove him nuts.

"I don't even have a boyfriend, and my mother is driving me insane." Harmony took another sip of her beer. "I can't imagine what she'll be like if I ever get engaged." She shuddered.

"Good luck with finding a single decent man in this town." Morticia poured more diet cola for herself.

"Right?" Harm shook her head. "I'd settle for single at this point. Trust me, I'm not picky. I just want someone to do life with. I mean you girls are great, but I get lonely. I'd love to have someone to cuddle up with and watch a movie or whatever."

"Get a cat," I said. "In my experience men are overrated. Only good for one thing, and you don't need a wedding to get that."

"You've just had bad luck, Tiff." Zoe looked pensive. "Maybe if you gave Matt—"

"Let me stop you right there, doll. That ship sailed when he made it clear I wasn't good enough for his family because I'm divorced."

"You're right, Tiff." I could tell the frustration was getting to Harm. "I don't need a wedding, but at this point, I can't even get a date night. I know I have a strong personality, but if I didn't know better, I would say the men in this town are avoiding me."

"Don't feel bad." Morti snorted. "On the rare occasion I get asked out on a date, I make a fool of myself. I am horrible at flirting and don't know how to talk to men, period." She shrugged. "My widowed father, on the other hand, has more game than I do. He is still dating a woman half his age. *Samantha.* At least he's not hiding her from me anymore."

"You both can do it. You just have to put yourself out there to get more comfortable around the opposite sex." Zoe always tried to see the silver lining.

"That's true, doll," I agreed, looking at Morti especially. "The only time you go out is with us."

"I interact with men." Morti smoothed back a strand of

black hair that had escaped her usual bun. "In fact, I just did this morning in that thriller book club I'm in."

"Cyber flirting doesn't count, Morti." Harm ran a frustrated hand through her red spiked hair. "Especially when you use an alias."

"Safety first," Morti replied weakly.

We all just stared at her.

"Oh, I know you're right." She huffed out a breath. "It's just hard. The real me is boring and a little freaky, or so I'm told. It's just easier online. I really want children, and I'm running out of time."

"You don't need a wedding for that, either." I patted my tummy.

"I know that. I just never pictured myself as a single mother." She shrugged. "Although, I'm not sure I can even have children."

"Medical advancements have come such a long way." Zoe squeezed Morti's hand. "Don't give up hope."

"I know, you're right. I just sometimes feel like my life is passing me by, and I'm going to end up with nothing to show for it."

"Well, this has turned into one downer of an evening." Harmony pouted.

"Then I'd say it's time we turned things right side up." Zoe put on classic rock music and started to dance.

"Now you're talking." Harm jumped up and joined her.

Morti rolled her eyes when they grabbed her hands

and pulled her to the dance floor, but she didn't protest as much as normal. I laughed and joined them...

Then, ten minutes later, I wet my pants and burst into tears.

THE NEXT DAY I walked into *Peace, Love, and Harmony*. The shop was filled with New Age trinkets, incense burning candles, and old books.

Harmony stood behind the counter, getting her cash register drawer ready for the day. She wore her "Where's the Beef" t-shirt and a pair of ripped jeans. Her auburn hair was extra gelled and spiked this morning. She looked up when I walked through the door, and the bell above it chimed.

Her face lit up, but almost as quickly, she sobered. "Tiff, what are you doing here? Don't get me wrong, babe, I'm thrilled to see you. Just making sure you're okay. Should I call McShamrock?"

"Definitely not."

"Well, you don't look so good, and he's the closest thing to family you've got." She picked up her phone, looking ready to dial someone. Anyone.

"I'm fine, Harm, really. I'm just restless. Anxious almost. That's why I'm here." I looked around her shop. "What can you give me to help?"

"Oh, well, that's normal."

"How would you know?"

"Are you kidding? I have seven brothers with several sisters-in-law, and too many nieces and nephews to count."

"True." I took a deep breath.

"That's it. Just keep taking deep breaths while I find you something." She looked over her supplies. "Okay, so first of all, I have some lavender essential oil to help calm and relax you. Mix a few drops with some witch hazel and some distilled water then spray it on your pillow to help you sleep. I can mix it into a small roller bottle for you and you can apply it directly to your wrists as needed. You can also put some in a diffuser to fill whatever room you're in with its scent."

"That sounds wonderful. I know I'll be up all the time once the twins are born, but I'm up all the time now having to pee. Not to mention, my thoughts are keeping me awake at night. Is this nature's way of preparing me for what's to come?"

Harmony laughed, holding up the lavender. "From what I've heard, yes, in part, but I can tell you, this will help ease your symptoms for sure."

"Thank you. You're a goddess. Zoe might know about babies, but she doesn't know anything about homeopathic remedies. That's why I came to you. Please, help me, doll. Give me more."

Harm tapped her short fingernails on the counter. "I've got it!" She went to a shelf behind her and pulled out an egg-sized crystal. "I have this blue celestite geode crystal, which is a rock that's cut in half, and it's crystalized on the inside."

"It's so pretty." I stared at the rock in awe. I'd always been drawn to sparkly, shiny things. "What does it do?"

"Well, the outer edge looks like a rock, but the crystals formed on the inside are a nice calming blue. They give off soft, serene vibrations that soothe and comfort the spirit. It enhances one's inner wisdom and grants direct access to the angelic realm."

The crystal looked wonderful, but I was confused. "What does that do for me?"

"This crystal releases energies of tranquility and peace. It's ideal for seeking harmony and connection."

"Harm, speak English." I bit back my frustration.

"Basically, it will help to balance your throat chakra. So, if you hold it in your hand," she held the twinkling geode in front of me, and I naturally took it as she continued, "it will calm any disruptions that produce anxiety for you and will help you to be more compassionate and understanding. It will also help you with verbalizing what you're feeling to others."

"I'll take it." Oddly enough I felt connected almost immediately upon holding it, and when I handed it back, I was surprised when I noticed an absence of calming energy.

"I thought you would." She winked and packaged up my possessions.

I grabbed my purse. "What do I owe you?"

"Nothing. It's my contribution to the bear cubs."

I laughed, and then my eye was drawn to a silver, foil-covered book with an intricate design on the spine. "What is that?" I pointed.

Harmony turned around and pulled the book from its shelf. "I'm not really sure. It came in on the last shipment. I put everything out for purchase, but I haven't really looked closely at the books yet. I ordered books on ancient myths and legends, as well as strange cults, etc. Why?" She looked at the cover closer. "Oh, wow, look at this." She pointed to the spine. "Doesn't that look like a...."

"A clover. Yes. That's what drew my eye." I took the book from her, and sure enough, there was a bright green four-leaf clover etched on the spine.

"What do you think it means?" A wary expression crossed her face.

"I don't know, but the clover kind of freaks me out, doll." I flipped the book open and started to skim the pages. I came to a spot that made me freeze in place.

"What? Did you find something?" Harmony's eyes grew wide.

My jaw fell open as I said in barely more than a whisper, "Yes." I looked up at her. "I found the Children of the Clover."

"What the hell does that mean?" Her face twisted into a look of horror. "It sounds terrifying. Like some scary movie."

"It might as well be. There is an ancient cult of men who think they are so superior; they want to preserve their line for all eternity."

Harmony barked out a laugh. "Yeah right. How are they going to do that?"

My eyes met hers. "By becoming seed spreaders."

"Seed...whaters?"

"They believe the four-leaf clover is so rare and special that they tattoo it on their penises, and then they target women to procreate with to spread their seed and keep the children to populate the Clover Clan."

Her jaw unhinged. "Dude, that is crazy weird."

I stared at her with determination...or obsession. I couldn't really tell what I looked like. "And yet suddenly makes so much sense."

She narrowed her eyes. "What does this have to do with you?"

"Apparently, an older woman is at the peak of her prime in wisdom and still fertile. And a forty-year-old woman is even better because she possesses the power of the four, producing children who are worthy enough to carry on the power of the Clover Legacy."

"Wait a minute, you think Matt McGinnis is a member of this cult?" Harmony gaped at me with major skepticism.

"How else would you explain the rumored legend? I saw something that looked suspiciously like a clover, and he got me pregnant on my fortieth birthday, with twins no less. Apparently, I'm very fertile but not so wise."

"Tiffany, I think the pregnancy hormones are talking." She patted my hand. "That's a bit of a stretch if you ask me."

"Well, I didn't." I tossed the book on my pile, feeling hysteria bubble up inside of me once more. "Add this to my order." I set my jaw. "I've got an egg-shaped geode to hold and some reading to do."

Chapter Nine

I sat at a table for two by the window in Lolita's Place, waiting for my sister, Tabatha, to join me. I'd been the bigger person and had asked her to meet me for lunch to talk. After all, she was as much a victim of all of this as I was. I'd never blamed her for our parents keeping her and giving me away.

It wasn't her fault any more than it was mine.

My heart beat faster when I saw her outside the window as she walked through the front door, spotted me, straightened her spine and then walked my way. She didn't say a word until she sat down and draped her napkin over her lap.

Our waitress came over and we placed our orders, then sat in awkward silence.

We might be identical twins, but we were different enough in most ways. She had the same golden-blonde hair as me, but hers was a short bob, and she wore blue jeans, which I had never worn in my life. The one truly identical thing about us was our periwinkle blue eyes, so like our mother's.

Inhaling deep, I smiled wide. "Hi, Tabatha."

"Tiffany." She didn't smile back.

"I'm so glad you decided to join me for lunch." I took in her stiff posture and tight face. "I didn't think you were going to. What changed your mind?"

She shrugged. "Mom."

"Ah, Rita." I nodded, refusing to call her *mom*. "I'm coming to realize she can be quite persuasive."

"*Mom* doesn't have an agenda," she leveled me with a hard stare, "if that's what you're thinking."

"Well, how would I know that?" I stared right back, locking gazes and refusing to blink first. "I really don't know the woman at all."

She looked away first as the waitress brought our food to the table, speaking only after the woman was gone. "You don't know me, either."

"And that's the reason for this lunch."

We took a moment to eat in silence.

"I want to get to know you, Tabatha." I set my napkin down. "We're sisters. Twins, for God's sake." My hand fluttered down over my stomach.

"I heard you were pregnant." Her gaze briefly followed my hand before she winced and looked away. "Congratulations. You and your husband must be thrilled."

"Thank you. No husband."

"Boyfriend then."

I shook my head. "No boyfriend, either, but yes. The father is very proud and surprisingly happy to be a father. I wasn't sure he would be."

"Being a parent is a gift."

"So, I'm told, but I didn't exactly have the best role models."

"Well, I did." She thrust her chin in the air.

I ignored the challenge and said carefully, "Now that I'm having twins of my own, I can't imagine them not being in each other's lives."

She let out a harsh laugh and shook her head at me. "We weren't in your life for lack of trying on *our* part."

"I didn't say I wanted Rita and Charlie in my life, but you are innocent in all of this. You didn't choose to be kept any more than I chose to be given away."

"You weren't given away. You were *taken* away." Tabatha threw up her hands. "I know you don't want to believe this, but Eugenia didn't keep her word and give you back like she was supposed to."

I was already shaking my head. "*Grammy* wouldn't do that." I couldn't go there. Because if I believed everything Tabatha and Rita were telling me, then the woman who raised me was a fraud, and I never really knew her at all. "She was the only one who has been there for me through everything I've gone through."

"What you've gone through?" Tabatha gaped at me. "That's a joke. You don't have any idea what real hardship looks like."

Her words cut through me. She didn't know anything

about me, so how could she judge me like this? I tried to put myself in her shoes and keep calm. "I heard about your husband and daughter's tragic death. I can't imagine what that was like. I didn't even know you were married. But you're not the only one who has been through shit. We all have had our battles, some more than others, but battles nonetheless."

"I can't do this. I told Mom I would try, but you have led a privileged life while we have struggled every day."

"Clearly, I can't either. This town loved Grammy, but I have been treated like a leech she had pity on. My cheating, manipulating, mentally abusive ex-husband—yes, I was married, too—only ever wanted me for my money. Still does. Other men have only ever wanted me for my looks, but those will fade in time."

Tabatha grunted but didn't say a word.

"Yes, Grammy took me in and loved me like her own, thank God, because my own parents didn't want me. Do you know how that feels? No, you don't. On top of all that, they robbed me of you, my only sibling, so don't tell me I haven't been through shit. And now that the only person who ever really gave a damn about me is gone, everyone is coming out of the woodwork wanting something from me. Well, I've had enough."

"Good, I guess we're finally on the same page." She stood.

"Apparently so. I thought maybe you would be different as my twin, but I'm not about to beg anyone to want to be a part of my life." I signaled for the check.

She opened her purse.

"Oh, don't bother. I'm Ms. Moneybags, remember? I don't need anything, especially not your money." I threw down a wad of cash, willing my tears not to fall, as I stood and looped my purse over my shoulder.

Her gaze met mine, and she hesitated a moment, her mouth opening as if she wanted to say something. I saved her the trouble and turned on my heel, marching my way out the door first. Somehow *her* not wanting me cut deeper than the others.

Just once I had thought that maybe, just maybe, I would be enough for someone.

It was the end of July, and I was twelve weeks along. No more morning sickness, thank the Lord, but I did have on my very first pair of granny panties and maternity pants. Zoe had been right. They really weren't that bad. My stomach had just started to thicken, and I couldn't stand anything tight pressing on it.

"And how is my favorite patient feeling today?" Dr. Joy walked into the exam room of the practice she shared with Chaz.

"I bet you say that to all of your patients," I grumbled, knowing I sounded like a pouting child but not being able to stop myself.

She laughed. "I see someone is experiencing pregnancy hormones." She checked the vitals her nurse had recorded.

"And then some," I admitted. "At least my morning sickness is gone finally. That was awful...times two!"

"Well, everything looks great on paper. We did your first sonogram at eight weeks. Now that you're twelve weeks, I'd like to do another one."

"Why, is something wrong?"

"It's just a precaution because you're having twins. Nothing to worry about, we just monitor you a little more closely." She pulled a machine closer to the table I sat on. "I'll just have you lie back, and we'll take a look."

I did as I was told, and then I heard a commotion outside the exam room door. Suddenly, in walked Matthew McGinnis, larger than life and scarier than ever. To my emotional state of mind anyway.

"Matt?" I sputtered. "What are you doing here?" I couldn't stop thinking that he might be a part of some crazy clover cult.

"Excuse me, sir." Dr. Joy frowned. "You can't just barge into an exam room when the door is closed."

"Chaz told me about the sonogram." His gaze locked onto mine, silencing any protest I might give, almost daring me to tell him to leave.

"Dr. Anderson shouldn't be talking about patients to anyone, let alone patients who aren't his." Dr. Joy crossed her arms over her lab coat and tapped her foot at Chaz, as he appeared by Matt's side, out of breath.

"Sorry, Tiffany." He looked apologetically at Dr.

Joy before he scowled at Matt. "I did not tell Mr. McGinnis about your sonogram today. He was asking me about twin pregnancies in general, and how often sonograms were done. I told him it depended on the mother, but we typically do them every four weeks in our office."

"Tiffany told me at eight weeks that she had a sonogram, and the twins were confirmed. I did the math and knew she was twelve weeks now." Matt's gaze swung back to mine. "It wasn't too hard to find out when yer appointment was today. Yer office isn't exactly discreet, if that's what ye were counting on." He narrowed his eyes at me, almost as if he felt hurt in some way. "What I want to know is why ye didn't tell me about yer sonogram today? I'm the babies' father. I have a right to know. Not to mention, did ye ever think maybe I would want to be present?"

He acted like he genuinely cared about his babies already. That was a first for me and was confusing me. Maybe he wasn't part of a cult, but I had to be sure. I didn't know I was having a sonogram today. I thought it was just another checkup. But he had a right to be involved if he wanted to.

"You're right," I finally said, coming to a decision.

He blinked. "I am?"

"As long as you're okay with him being here, Tiffany, then I've got my own patients waiting." Chaz raised a brow at me, waiting for my confirmation.

I nodded. "Matt can stay."

Chaz tipped his head once and then closed the door behind him.

"Well, Mr. McGinnis, you won't be finding out the sex of the babies until twenty weeks, if that's what you're hoping for by being here." Dr. Joy gestured for him to stand on the other side of me where he could still see the monitor as she performed the sonogram.

"I don't care what sex the babies are. I just want to see them with me own eyes." He watched her squeeze a jelly type substance onto my stomach and roll a wand around until images popped up on the screen. "Make sure they're okay."

I studied his face and the sincerity written all over it. He really did care about his children already, I thought, surprised. When a look of wonder transformed his features, I turned my head to stare at the monitor and my jaw unhinged. The 3D ultrasound was in full color. I couldn't get over the detail of how developed a twelve-week-old fetus already was.

We could see both babies, and it was like nothing I had ever experienced.

All of a sudden, I felt a hand squeeze mine. I glanced up at Matt and saw tears in his eyes at the same time that I felt my cheeks grow wet. Something happened between us, and I felt a bond grow. At this moment nothing else mattered. We would forever be connected to each other through our children.

I'd never had an "our" anything before.

"Okay, Mom and Dad, your babies look great. I'll see

you back in four weeks for another sonogram. And four weeks after that you can decide if you want to know the sex."

"Yes," I said.

"No," Matt said simultaneously.

Dr. Joy looked back and forth between the two of us. "Like I said, you have time to decide. In the meantime, you've made it through the scariest part of the pregnancy. The first trimester. Feel free to tell anyone you haven't already."

"In this town, everyone knows everything," I said.

"That's fer sure," Matt agreed.

"Okay, well, I suggest you start planning your nursery, buying baby clothes, figuring out a schedule, etc." Dr. Joy made some notes on her computer. "The babies will be here before you know it."

I could feel my face pale.

"We're on it, Doc." Matt spoke up when it was clear I couldn't.

Dr. Joy finished up, and Matt didn't leave until I did. He walked me out of the exam room and through the packed waiting room, causing all eyes to focus on us. *Great.* Gerty and Gabby Rogers raised brows at us, while Bitsy's hand fluttered over her stomach as if just being in my presence might cause her harm.

I sighed.

"Come on, lass." Matt rested his hand at the small of my back as he steered me outside. "Let's get ye out of here."

I allowed him to lead me outside because I didn't have the energy to put up a fight. Once we hit the parking lot, I dug in my heels as reality set back in. What was his agenda? Did he really have a clover tattoo? Had he been mad because he'd gotten caught? Had he not used protection on purpose, hoping to get me pregnant because he'd found out it was my fortieth birthday? Had his proposal been a sham to throw me off? Did he plan to fight for custody and get rid of me after they were born?

I squeezed my eyes tight and shook my head hard, trying to stop myself from spiraling. "I appreciate what you were trying to do back there, Matt, but I'm a big girl. I can handle whatever this town throws at me on my own."

"Why when ye don't have to? Yer not alone, Tiffany." He looked me in the eyes with an honesty even I couldn't deny. Or he was a really good actor. "Ye have me."

"Look, I know we're connected through our babies, but that's it," I said firmly. "There is no us."

He ran a hand through his curls. "Aye, yer a stubborn lass."

I thrust my finger in his face. "You should talk."

He dropped his hands to his hips and just stared at me. Finally, he scrubbed a hand over his jaw. "Okay, then. I'll make ye a proposition. There is no us, but ye agree I can be a part of our children's lives."

I frowned. "We've already been over this. Of course you can be a part of our children's lives. I would never deny them that." But I would be secretly watching him like a mama bear. If he tried to take my cubs, I'd be taking care of him...permanently.

"Starting now," he said, pulling me from my thoughts.

"What do you mean, starting now?" I eyed him carefully, taking a step back and kicking myself for it. "They're not even here yet."

"Sure, they are. They're in yer belly, and ye need help whether ye like it or not." He pointed at me.

My mouth gaped, but I couldn't really deny what he was saying. It had been obvious at the doctor's office that I was in over my head. I crossed my arms over my chest. "What would this proposition look like?"

He slid his hands in his jeans' pockets. "I want to go with ye to yer doctor's appointments. I will help ye buy all the baby clothes, supplies, and furnishings. And I will be here for ye anytime ye need to talk, rant, cry, laugh...whatever. I happen to be a great listener with plenty of nieces and nephews fer experience. Let's just say I know a thing or two about women and babies."

I bet he did, I thought as my suspicions about Children of the Clover came flooding back, but I thought about everything he said. He had a big family. I didn't. He had nieces and nephews. I didn't. He had experience. I didn't.

I had my best friends, but they had their own busy lives. I already bothered them enough, even though they say I'm never a bother. I knew they would do anything for me, but I had to learn how to do this on my own. And the children were half Matt's, after all.

The saying, *Keep your friends close and your enemies closer*, came to me.

I nodded once. "Okay, on one condition."

"What's that?"

"No romance. We are strictly soon-to-be co-parents."

"Deal, but I'd like to think we're also friends." His eyes softened.

"Friends." I tested the word. Or frenemies? Either way, I planned to keep my eye on him which left me with only one answer, "Deal."

Chapter Ten

That evening, after a full day of shopping all things baby with Matt, I headed to Maple Ridge Market for groceries because I had no food in my apartment. I usually ate out, but I figured that wasn't the healthiest. Besides, I had to get used to cooking for my children. I stumbled while pushing my shopping cart over that thought.

Let's just say men weren't drawn to me for my culinary skills.

Grammy had a chef, housekeepers, groundskeepers, a chauffeur, and more. I never really knew what it was like to live a normal life. I was determined to bring my children up to be well-rounded, humble, kind, and self-sufficient. They needed to be able to relate to all sorts of people, and most importantly, be able to take care of themselves.

Zoe had given me tips, like shopping on the outskirts of the store for fresh, non-processed foods and a list of ingredients to buy. I traveled halfway around the store when I finally reached the health food specialty section.

My heart skipped a beat when I saw a man with a jar of honey in his hands. I thought it was Matt for a moment, but he was already at McGinny's Pub, getting ready for the dinner crowd. I looked closer. The man was smaller than Matt and younger, but not by much. Other than that, they looked just alike.

He glanced up at me and smiled wide. "Hey, there. Yer me cousin's fiancée, right? I'm Aidan."

"I'm not his fiancée."

"Wait, girlfriend then?"

"No."

"But aren't ye having his babies?"

"Yes."

"Ohhh." His eyes grew wide and then glanced briefly at my H brooch before snapping back up to mine. "Sorry, I thought I heard he proposed. I didn't realize ye said no."

"First of all, he didn't propose." I set my jaw. "He *ordered* me to marry him, to which I firmly let him know I can take care of myself."

Aidan grinned wide, revealing the same set of dimples as Matt. "Aye, I can see why he likes you, lass."

I rolled my eyes and then my gaze locked on the product in his hands. "I-Is that *clover* honey?"

"Absolutely. Clovers are full of antioxidants, they're good fer the heart, and help with digestion. Matt always uses them in his recipes. He sent me here to fetch some clover honey and sprouts."

Hmmm, I was pretty sure I'd witnessed a sprouting clover firsthand. "I take it clovers are pretty special to your family."

"Well, we are Irish, after all." He winked. "Most people see shamrocks, which are only green with three leaves. Clovers can be four leaves and either purple or green. They're rare and special. If ye see a four-leaf clover, especially the purple ones, consider yourself lucky."

Matt's four-leaf clover looked purple, if memory served me correctly, but considering his wasn't made by nature, I didn't feel lucky. I felt deceived and worried. The evidence was stacking up in favor of him being a part of that crazy cult.

I cleared my throat. "So, um, do you have any tattoos?" *Like, say, a particular clover tattoo?* I thought as I studied him.

"Oh, no, me mum would tan me hide." He shook his head.

"Smart woman," I muttered.

"Speaking of tanning hides, I'd better get these back to Matt before he tans mine." Aidan shot me a wave over his shoulder and said as he walked away, "Yer a good egg, Ms. Eisenhower. Take care of me cousins."

Cousins? Oh, the babies. "Don't you worry, Aidan. I won't let them get tattoos of *any* kind, either. You can mark my words on that one," I hollered back, more suspicious than ever. I had to do something to find out for sure, and there was only one way I could think of to do that.

I needed to get a closer look at that clover tattoo.

A WHILE later after I finished my grocery shopping, I pulled into the parking lot of my store and apartment. I grabbed a couple bags and walked around front to the porch, which had an entrance to my spa and a separate entrance to my apartment upstairs. I froze in my tracks and stared at the man before me.

"What are you doing here, Bud?" I ground my teeth to keep from saying what I really wanted to.

After all, the man was suing me yet again. It wasn't like we shared children. *He* was the child. Constantly faking injuries, telling lies about me, and claiming I'm the reason he's hurt and can't work. That I owe him and can settle that debt by paying him more money.

"I'm here to see you, babe." He grabbed his back as he stood. "I would help you with those grocery bags, but my back is bad...as you know."

I set the bags down. I wasn't about to unlock my door until he left. "You're not getting any more money from me, and I don't want to see you."

"Oh, I think a judge will have something else to say about that." He took a menacing step toward me.

I fought the urge to take a step back. I wasn't wearing high heels this time, so he was slightly taller than me...and definitely stronger.

"Lucky for me I inherited Grammy's attorneys as well. I really don't think you want to mess with Victoria Steele and Alexandra Knight of The Steely Knight Agency."

His face paled slightly at the mention of their names. He was a male chauvinist by nature, but even he knew of their reputation for being ruthless and brutal. They would eat him alive and not think twice about it.

"Don't you worry. My family has pull in this town." His face looked smug.

I laughed. "Your family doesn't want anything to do with you because you're a loser. They only cared when you were married to me because they knew I would one day inherit Grammy's money, same as you. None of you ever wanted me, and now I want nothing to do with any of you."

His gaze locked onto the grocery bag with newborn diapers inside, and I silently cursed. He would find out sooner or later, I had just hoped it would be later.

"You're pregnant," he ground out, sounding less than thrilled, probably because he didn't want to share my inheritance with anyone. "I thought you hated kids."

"I never said I hated children. I was just afraid I wouldn't be a good mother." I realized I said that out loud and snapped my spine straight.

"Aren't you too old to have a baby?" He snorted with a twisted grin.

"Apparently not, since I'm having *babies*," I said with emphasis, relishing in the shocked look on his face that had replaced his grin.

"Who's the poor bastard you tricked into that one?" He snorted.

A shadow blocked out the setting sun, covering us both.

"That would be me, laddy, and if yer not very careful in how ye talk to a lady, I'll show ye what a poor bastard really looks like."

At six foot five, Matt towered over Bud, and he was twice as muscular. I'd never seen that look on Matt's face before, and I never wanted to be on the receiving end of it. It was quite comical watching Bud's face pale considerably.

Bud held up his hands before him. "Dude, all I'm trying to do is get what is rightfully mine."

"Let me be perfectly clear, *dude*. Absolutely nothing about Ms. Eisenhower belongs to ye. Understood?"

Bud stuck his chest out, but suddenly he didn't look as strong as I remembered. "You'll be hearing from my lawyer."

Matt's grin looked downright intimidating. "I don't need a lawyer to win or a court to pass judgement."

Bud took a step back, eying him warily. "Is that a threat?"

Matt briefly flexed his chest, which even made Bud take notice. "That's a promise, laddy. I suggest ye heed me warning while ye still can."

Matt's hands were balled loosely into massive fists, and he took a step forward. Bud jumped backward and fell off my porch. He scrambled to his feet and his gaze shot quickly to me.

"This conversation isn't over, Tiff." Bud bolted down the street, not looking injured in the least.

I looked at Matt. "Thank you, but what are you doing here? Aren't you supposed to be at the pub?"

"I was at the pub, and then I saw yer porch from me office window. I knew who he was from yer grandmother's funeral. Not that ye needed me help or anything. I know how ye hate that. But I just thought I would make sure everything was okay."

"Well, thank you for that. I really do appreciate it." I picked up my bags, and Matt immediately took them from me. I looked at him with a raised eyebrow.

"For me babies."

I shook my head, but didn't argue, too tired to do anything but unlock my door. I stepped inside and climbed the stairs to the apartment above my spa, just now realizing how difficult this was going to be once I was hugely pregnant with twins.

I frowned.

Matt followed me up, carrying both bags easily. "Aidan said he saw ye at the grocery store earlier." He set the bags on the counter. "Is that all ye bought?"

"No, the rest is in my car. I didn't want to unlock my place until Bud was gone." I slipped my shoes off and rubbed my lower back.

"Have a seat and don't do anything. I'll be right back." Matt disappeared.

I looked at the groceries, contemplating putting them away, but my back ached, and my feet were killing me already. It had been a long day. I would put them away in a minute. I just needed a second off my feet. I sat on my couch and closed my eyes.

It felt like only minutes passed by.

A strong sensation that someone was watching me had my eyelids fluttering open. Matt sat staring at me from the chair next to the sofa I was lying on. Somehow, I was lying down and a blanket was draped over me.

I glanced around. All of the groceries were put away and the sun had set.

I sat up. "How long was I out?"

He glanced at his watch. "About an hour."

I gaped at him. "Why didn't you wake me?"

He shrugged. "Ye obviously needed the sleep."

"You didn't have to put my groceries away." I was decidedly uncomfortable that he had watched me sleep. It made me feel vulnerable. I folded the blanket and draped it back over the couch.

"Ye had perishable items. Besides, I didn't mind." He stared at me as he paused a beat. "That's what friends do."

"Well, thank you, but I imagine you have to get back to the pub, don't you?" I stood and went into the kitchen to make myself a cup of tea.

He followed me and sat at my table. "Aidan has it covered. It's good for him to be on his own for a bit. Besides, Finn is singing tonight, so he'll let me know if I'm needed."

"Care for something to drink?" I felt the need to ask after all he had done.

"Tea is good."

I raised a brow. "Really?"

"I love a good cup of tea."

"All I have is caffeine-free herbal tea. I hope that's okay."

"Do you have any honey?"

I blinked and then carefully said, "I do, but just normal honey."

"Is there any other kind?" He laughed.

This was my opening. "Funny you should ask." I handed him the steaming cup and a jar of honey. "Aidan was in the health food section when I ran into him. He said you asked him to pick up clover honey. You must really like clovers."

He arched a brow and just stared at me. "Clovers are very healthy."

"Don't forget rare and special." I pursed my lips.

"Well, the four-leaf ones, yes," he said flatly.

"The kind that would make for a great tattoo...if you were into that sort of thing, of course."

"So, I've heard." He sipped his tea, which was growing colder by the minute, while studying me over the rim of the cup.

"Aidan said clovers are a big deal to your family."

"Did he now?" Matt set his cup down.

"Aidan said his mother wouldn't approve of him getting any tattoos. Just so you know, I won't approve of our kids getting any tattoos either, especially if they are boys?" I didn't mind tattoos at all, but he didn't need to know that. I wanted to make sure he wouldn't recruit our children into the Children of the Clover cult. If he was a member, that is.

The jury was still out.

"Don't ye think it's a little early to worry about our children getting a tattoo? Why don't we let them be born before we add that to the list of things to stress out about."

"Do you have any tattoos?" I tried to ask as casually as I could.

"I know what yer trying to do, but fer the life of me I can't figure out why." He stood. "I told ye before that I wasn't going to verify the foolish legend one way or the other."

"I wasn't asking about that." I laughed and waved off his suspicions. "I just meant tattoos in general. Did your mother forbid you from getting any, like Aidan's did?"

"Aidan is still a lad." He locked eyes with mine. "I am not. I have the utmost respect for me ma, but she doesn't have a say in what I do."

That knocked the wind out of my sails. "Like having twins out of wedlock with a divorced, forty-year-old woman." My shoulders drooped and I set my cup in the sink, wondering if I would ever have his parents' approval.

"I didn't say that." His tone was gentle.

"You didn't deny it either," I responded quietly.

"I have to get going. Lock the door behind me, lass." He walked out the door, and I followed him, locking my apartment up tight. This is what I wanted. My independence. Being on my own. Navigating life by myself....

Then why did I feel so alone?

Chapter Eleven

Over the past two weeks, I hadn't seen or heard from Bud. I was hopeful this meant he was finally going to stay out of my life, but I was afraid to get my hopes up too much. I knew him too well. He was like a toddler. If he was quiet, then he was up to no good.

I just needed to figure out what that meant.

In the meantime, Matt had hardly left my side. It was like he anticipated my every need before I even knew I needed it. The few times that he was gone, he was either working at the pub or being strangely secretive about some mysterious outings. I asked him about it, but he simply said it was a surprise.

I hated surprises.

So, I stood outside of my apartment waiting for him to pick me up. It was mid-August, and I was fourteen weeks pregnant and hot as the dickens. A heatwave was passing through Mayflower, and I was *not* a fan.

I glanced at my watch. It was still morning. I'd already had breakfast, but my stomach was rumbling again. These babies were always hungry, but what did I expect, given who their father was?

Matt pulled up next to the curb in a massive pickup truck. Before I could even touch the door handle, he hopped out and jogged around the hood to open the door.

"You're late." I leveled a stare at him.

It must be nature's way to prepare a woman for motherhood by making her have to go to the bathroom all night long. Being sleep deprived, hungry, and hot all at the same time was making me cranky as a mama bear, and I didn't even have any cubs yet.

"Aye, lass, but when ye see what's inside, ye'll forgive me." He held out his hand and I slid mine into his as I stepped onto the foot running board. My sandal had barely touched the step when he gave my bottom a boost with his other hand.

I let out a little yelp, and he boomed a big hearty laugh of delight then closed the door with a resounding thud. The man was like a grizzly bear. He ran around the hood once more and slid into the driver's side with ease then held up a bag for me.

"What's that?" I eyed him curiously.

"A morning snack." He winked, and just like that, I forgave him.

The aroma wafting out of the bag had me salivating. I snatched the bag from him and peeked inside. Warm bagels with cream cheese, a cup of fruit, and herbal tea. I looked up at him with misty eyes as I sighed the words, "Have I told you lately that I love you?"

He blinked, his lips parting slightly.

My heart skipped a beat and I quickly added, "The babes love you, I mean." I laughed a little too hyena-ishly.

He chuckled. "Now that we've clarified that, are ye ready to find out what yer surprise is, lass?"

"At this point I would say *yes* to anything," I answered, before biting into my heavenly delight and moaning my appreciation.

"Music to me ears." He slid the gearshift into drive, and off we went.

Fifteen minutes later, on the outskirts of town, we pulled into the driveway of an adorable ranch. It was a dove gray with white trim and a lovely front porch. Matt cut the engine and hopped out of the truck, jogging around to open my door before I could even wipe my hands after my delicious snack. He placed his big hands on both sides of my waist and easily lifted me down, no running boards necessary.

"Thank you, but I'm not entirely helpless you know." I sighed.

"Sorry," he said with a grin. "Force of habit."

I rolled my eyes. "So, whose house are we at anyway?" I fanned my cheeks from the early morning heat already. It was going to be a hot one.

"Ours." Matt nodded once, looking very similar to when he'd proposed. No question, just stating a face as if it were set in stone.

My hand stopped moving, and my heart started to pound. "Excuse me?" Living with McShamrock was *not* an option.

"I have another proposition for ye." His eyes sparkled.

I dropped my arm to my side, letting my walls slide back into place to guard my heart. "Matt..."

He held up his hands. "It's not what ye think. Just hear me out, lass. Please? For the sake of the wee babes."

"The babes card? Really?"

He shrugged. "What can I say? I'm a desperate man."

He was sure something. I blew out a breath and crossed my arms while I still could. "Like I have a choice to do anything else. It's not like I'm going anywhere at the moment. No wonder you kept this a secret."

He ignored my response and dove right into his explanation. "Yer apartment is going to get a lot more difficult to climb those stairs when ye are in yer last trimester. Not to mention carrying two infant carriers up and down stairs plus diaper bags and strollers is going to be exhausting."

He had a point. I used to be able to jog up my stairs no problem, but lately, I was so winded by the time I reached the top. "I'm listening."

"So, I found this house fer rent. It's perfect. All on one floor, not too far from town, and it's four bedrooms. Plenty of room fer us all."

"Wait...there is no *us all*." My tummy fluttered, and I was pretty sure it wasn't the babies as I hadn't felt them move yet. "Besides, I don't take charity, and like I've said before, I am more than capable of providing for myself and the babies."

"Aye, lass, I'm not saying ye are not. Ye promised to hear me out, remember?" He looked me in the eyes with sparkling blue orbs I found hard to resist.

"Fine, go on."

He shrugged. "That's where me proposition comes in. I say we both rent out our apartments to friends or family members, while we move in here together and share the expenses fer one year. Then we can reevaluate at that time."

An entire year of living together?

I didn't know if I could resist him, let alone worrying about him resisting me. I cleared my throat. "I told you no romance." My words sounded weak to my own ears.

"And there won't be any," he said far too easily.

Why was I annoyed when this was my idea?

"I'm talking about co-parenting," he continued, oblivious to my inner turmoil. "It will be much easier fer us to help each other if we both live under the same roof, at least fer the first year. It's twins we're talking about, Tiffany. You can't do that on yer own. No one can. And I'm more than willing to help. In fact, I want to. They're my children too, and I don't want to miss out, so please say yes, love."

There went my heart again. He had no idea his simple terms of endearment melted my heart, but I knew that was just the way he talked. I took a deep breath and focused as I thought about everything he said. Once again, he was right. Middle of the night feedings. Diaper changes. Colic. Daytime baths. Pediatrician visits. Car rides....

Times two!!

Everything he said made sense.

I was lucky that he wanted to be so involved. It wasn't always like that for a lot of new mothers. I knew nothing about babies, and two of them just seemed overwhelming. For the first time, I could kind of understand how my mother must have felt. Even with my father on board, they hadn't been able to handle two babies.

What had I been thinking?

I hadn't, plain and simple. I simply didn't want my children to go through life feeling unwanted. I studied the man staring back at me with the utmost sincerity, and I really started to believe I didn't have to do that alone.

I nodded slowly. "Okay."

His eyes widened. "Yeah?"

I shook my head *no*, but said, "Yes." I switched to nodding the more I thought about the whole idea of platonic cohabitation. "That makes sense. No romance, and there are plenty of bedrooms to co-parent and still have our own lives," I said out loud, more for my benefit than his.

"Great!" He grinned wide and rubbed his large hands together. "I guess we're doing this thing then."

"I guess so...and sight unseen, no less." I laughed, trying not to let it turn into hysteria. "There will be ground rules to cohabiting, you know. I have certain standards to maintain and definite deal breakers."

"I would expect nothing less." He winked.

I blinked. "Um, okay then. Maybe I should actually see where I'm going to be living for the next year. Lead the way, Mr. McGinnis."

"Ye got it, lass."

I followed Matt, watching the way his body moved, and realized I might be in trouble in the *no romance* department. But then another thought came to me. If we shared a house, that gave me several months to answer one burning question...

Is the father of my babies a member of the Children of the Clover?

THAT FRIDAY NIGHT, I walked into Harmony's apartment above her New Age shop for girls' night. I was the last to arrive again, as usual. I'd never been very prompt, and especially now that I had *pregnancy brain*, my tardiness had gotten worse. There were times I couldn't even remember what day it was.

"There's our little mama," Harm said.

I grunted. "I'm not so little anymore." I bypassed the table and went straight to the couch, propping my feet up on her coffee table with a big sigh. "My clothes are getting too tight, and my feet are starting to swell. I'm only fifteen weeks, but with Big Foot as their father, I'm terrified to go full term."

Zoe brought me a plate of cheese, crackers, pepperoni,

fruit, celery, and blue cheese. She knew the chicken wings would give me heartburn, so she'd wisely skipped those. She handed me sparkling water in a fancy glass, and then joined me on the sofa. "Speaking of our favorite Irishman, how is it going with him helping you? I haven't received any 911 calls from you, so I'm assuming well?"

"Helping?" I choked on my water. "That's an understatement." I set my plate of snacks down and wiped my mouth before adding, "The man bought us a house."

"Wait, what?" Harm gaped at me, grabbing her beer and chicken wings as she made her way into her living room to sit in the recliner beside the couch. "You can't drop a bomb like that and not give us the full detes, so spill it, babe."

"Well, he didn't *buy* the house exactly." I took a bite of fruit as I rephrased what I wanted to say. "He rented it."

"Oh, I thought you meant you two were moving in together." Morticia laughed as she joined us with a diet cola and pizza and sat in another recliner on the other side of the couch. "Yeah, like that might happen over your dead body."

Everyone laughed except me.

"Then I must be dying because it's happening." I sighed, but the only thing that died was their laughter. "I'm just not very good at articulating things lately." I took a bite of cheese and crackers.

"But I thought you said you would only allow Matt to help you if there was no romance involved?" Zoe sipped her chardonnay, staring off in thought. "Moving in together sounds kind of romantic."

"I know, that's what I'm afraid of," I admitted. "But he did have some good points. We're going to have to start hosting our girls' night in our shops because I can't handle these stairs much longer. All of our homes, including Matt's, are in upstairs apartments. The only ones who don't live upstairs are Zoe and Chaz. So, Matt got the idea that if he rented a four-bedroom ranch, then we could each take one bedroom, leaving two to spare. That's plenty of room, and it's only for one year. Through the pregnancy and the first few months because there's no way I can handle two babies by myself."

"That actually makes sense." Zoe nodded.

"Good for you for allowing Matt to help you." Morti agreed. "You're so independent, I know it's hard for you to let someone in."

"Not just someone...her baby daddy." Harm wagged her eyebrows.

"And possible Children of the Clover member," I added.

Harm's eyes widened. "You're still on that crazy train?"

"Children of the what?" Zoe asked.

"Yeah, I'm confused." Morti scratched her head.

"You didn't tell them?" I looked at Harm.

"Um, no, because the whole idea is crazy." She held up her hands, always one to speak her mind and keep things real.

I knew she had her doubts, but I didn't. "I found a book

on this ancient cult in Harmony's shop. I was drawn to the book because of the clover on the cover.

"Clover?" Zoe blinked. "That sounds a little too coincidental."

"Right?" I set my feet down and scooted forward. "Basically, a long time ago, a group of men thought they were so fabulous, perfect specimens of the male gender. So much so that they tattooed their penises with a four-leaf clover and then spread their seed to special women. They especially felt that a woman who turned forty was superior in knowledge and still fertile. Then the babies became Children of the Clover, raised to carry on the legacy. Male babies were coveted the most for obvious reasons."

Morti eyed the other two before looking back at me. "I have to say I'm with Harm. The cult sounds a little too crazy to be true. I'm sure it's just some old legend. Probably where the legend of the tattooed clover penis sprouted from."

"Oh, it sprouted all right. I saw it with my own eyes. Well, I saw something, anyway, but Matt won't let me take another look."

"Gee, I can't imagine why." Zoe laughed on a wince. "You don't really believe this is true, do you?"

"I don't know." I threw my hands up in the air and flopped back on the cushions. "You guys make me feel like I've gone crazy. Who knows, maybe I have. All I know for certain is that I need to know for sure."

"Well, living with Matt is a step in the right direction." Harm snorted.

"My thoughts exactly." I nodded with determination. "Now I just have to figure out how to make that happen without seeming like a sex-crazed maniac."

"Good luck with that one," Zoe said knowingly.

"What does that mean?" I eyed her curiously.

"It's a pregnancy thing." Zoe giggled. "Now that your morning sickness is gone, you'll enter the horny phase, so a sex-crazed maniac isn't too far off."

My jaw unhinged.

Matt was already hard enough to resist. How the hell was I going to handle being horny while living with a gorgeous Thor lookalike? "Well, that's just great. I already signed on the dotted line."

"Something tells me good ole' McShamrock doesn't have a clue what *he* signed up for." Harmony laughed.

"And this is why online dating is my preferred choice," Morticia stated. "Cyber-sex is so much less stressful."

"But far less enjoyable, babe," Harmony countered.

"And it can't give you a baby," Zoe added gently.

"Or two." I groaned.

Maybe Matt's brilliant idea wasn't so brilliant after all.

Chapter Twelve

"Are you sure you want to rent the apartment upstairs?" I asked Trixy a week later as she sat behind the reception desk of my salon.

Matt's cousin, Finn, was taking over his apartment and letting Aidan stay with him. They'd been crashing at his uncle's house, who was more than happy to have them, but family was family. They knew Matt needed help, so they jumped in, no questions asked.

I didn't have that luxury.

Trixy nodded, and her bleach blonde pigtails bounced. "My parents are sick of having me live with them. Failure to launch, and all that." She laughed. "And since it's only for one year, it's a great trial run for me to see what it's like totally adulting on my own. I'm not gonna lie...I'm kinda nervous."

Trixy was in her late twenties, definitely not a kid anymore. She was a whiz at computers but pretty much clueless about everything else. Her parents had always helped her manage—more like taken over—everything else, but now they were ready for her to leave the nest and start her own life. I couldn't blame them, but I could also sympathize with her. I lived with my Grammy until I was in my mid-twenties, then went out on my own. I didn't regret anything except getting married.

But I never made the same mistake twice.

"You'll do great." I patted her hand. "Speaking of adulting, I have to finish packing. *I'm* not gonna lie...I'm *not* gonna miss climbing those stairs." I winked.

Trixy laughed. "I think it's great that you and Mr. McGinnis are moving in together. He's so hot."

"It's not like that between us." I sighed.

Here we go. It was only a matter of time before the rumor mill started, and Trixy wasn't the first. Tongues had been wagging since the moment we signed on the dotted line to rent the ranch.

Her face puckered up. "But aren't you having his babies?"

And there it was.

I inhaled and counted to ten. "Yes, but we're not a couple."

"If you say so." Her eyes twinkled.

I rolled mine. "We're moving in together to co-parent, that's all."

"That's good. I'm glad you'll have someone to help you. Twins are a lot, and Matt's like...huge."

In more ways than one, I thought. "You have no idea."

Her eyes widened. "Oh, my God, I can't imagine giving birth to one—let alone two—of his babies." She shuddered.

"You and me both." I could feel my anxiety heighten just thinking about it.

Trixy's gaze landed on me as realization dawned. "Oh, I'm so sorry. You'll be fine, I'm sure. Good childbearing hips, and all."

Well, that certainly didn't make me feel any better.

I was officially four months and so not feeling fabulous to begin with. My hips were definitely starting to widen as my organs shifted around to make room for the Sasquatch twins. Damn Zoe for giving me a book on what to expect while I was expecting.

I'd come to the conclusion there were some things I just didn't want to know.

"I mean..." Trixy's face looked stricken.

"It's okay, really." I slowed my breathing and forced those terrifying thoughts from my mind. "The apartment will be ready for you in a few days."

"Sounds good. I don't have much to pack since you're leaving the place furnished. Thank you for that."

"Matt and I both decided we would leave our personal things at our own apartments and just pick up new things together for our shared space. We're each just bringing along the essentials and a few favorite items. Nothing crazy, just enough to get by while we figure out how to raise twins together. This is a trial run for us as well."

"Well, that's smart. I promise to take good care of your things while you're away playing house." She smiled wide.

"I wouldn't have asked you if I thought otherwise." I winked. "Well, I guess I'd better head to Maple Ridge Market. I have literally no food in my refrigerator, and these babies can eat."

"I bet." Trixy chuckled. "I'll hold down the fort here. Lucy and Maxim are booked solid, but the rest of your day is free. Enjoy it."

"Thanks, Trixy. What would I do without you?"

"Nothing, because you're never getting rid of me." She winked back.

I headed out the door and ran into Truman Winters, ambling down the street with his mailbag, just as he arrived at my mailbox.

"Hi, Truman. Any rain in the forecast?" I looked at the clear blue sky, knowing that didn't matter one bit. Truman was the real weather predictor.

"Oh, there's a storm a brewin', but it ain't in the form of rain." He pushed his coke-bottle glasses back up his nose and looked at me with sympathy.

What now?

His voice sounded so serious; I was almost afraid to ask. After an awkward moment of silence, I tilted my head. "How do you mean?"

He handed me a certified letter.

I groaned. No words were necessary.

Since our divorce five years ago, Bud had sued me at least once a year. Sometimes he used a service that gave me the court papers in a manilla envelope. Other times he went the cheaper route and sent a certified letter through the mail carrier.

Bud couldn't get over me being the one to leave him. His ego was too big for that. So now all he wanted to do was get back at me any chance he could.

"Sorry, Tiffany, but looks like you've been served again." Truman shook his head as he handed me a pen, and I signed for the letter.

If I didn't sign, the letter would be returned to Bud, and he would have to start over. But that would just delay the inevitable, so why bother? He wouldn't go away. He never did. I couldn't take much more of this, and now I had a family to think about. I was sick of his lies and games.

I had to find a way to prove he was a fraud for good this time.

"It's okay." I patted the mail carrier's arm. "You're just doing your job. All Bud cares about is winning, but the fool never does."

And I wasn't about to let him this time.

AFTER STORING the letter in my apartment, I headed to Maple Ridge Market.

Looked like I wasn't the only one who didn't like to cook. The place was busy with a bunch of people picking up something for dinner, judging by the amount of people in front of the meals-to-go counter.

Zoe had offered to teach me how to cook. I was thinking more and more about taking her up on it. After all, I had more than myself to think about these days. Every time I thought about becoming a mother, I was terrified.

What if I was horrible at it?

Yes, Grammy raised me, but she wasn't exactly the motherly type. I'd never had that. I knew she loved me, but her staff did most of the mothering. Honestly, even though I had the money for it, I wasn't sure I wanted that for my children.

Deciding to be better at this, I turned my cart around and headed to the produce section. At least I knew how to make a salad. I would start by feeding myself, and hopefully by the time the twins were born, I would be better at feeding them home-cooked meals.

All of a sudden, my stomach fluttered.

I jerked to a halt. Was that hunger pains?

I felt it again on the other side. Oh, God, was I going into premature labor? I started breathing faster but couldn't quite get enough air. I'd never planned to have children, had never really wanted any, and now I couldn't imagine not having them in my life.

How could I have grown to love human beings I hadn't even met yet? I bent over my cart and kept trying to suck in breath. I was going to lose my babies and then die right here in the middle of Maple Ridge Market.

That would certainly give this town something to talk about.

Everything started to darken. I was about to pass out. Suddenly, I felt a presence.

A gentle voice beside me said, "Take slow deep breaths," as they held a paper bag in front of my face. I took it and focused on breathing into it as they rubbed my back soothingly.

I blinked the tears from my eyes. *Rita?*

I looked to the side and sure enough, my mother stood there calmly but firmly, and I did as I was told without question, feeling comforted almost immediately. Several minutes later, my breathing returned to normal, and she pulled the bag away.

"Better?" Her eyes were filled with understanding and kindness.

Her short blonde hair was mixed with gray in a simple, stylish cut, and she wore a blue sundress, a shade paler than her periwinkle eyes. She was nothing like Grammy had described. I didn't know what to think anymore. She looked innocent and sweet, and since I'd met her, she'd been nothing but kind.

And it confused the hell out of me.

"Yes, much," I finally responded.

"Good. Let's sit on this bench for a bit just to be sure you're okay." She led me and my cart to a bench along the wall by the lottery ticket machines.

I stifled a hysterical giggle.

Who would have thought my mother showing up would be my lucky day? I looked down at my stomach, feeling what she must have felt forty years ago when she was pregnant with me and Tabatha. I felt connected to her, and I didn't want to. Or did I?

I just didn't know what I wanted anymore.

It felt like a betrayal to Grammy if I allowed myself to have a relationship with my parents and sister, but was it really? Did Grammy lie to me for my entire life? If that were true, that would be my breaking point.

"Thank you." My voice was barely more than a whisper as it pushed its way past the lump in my throat.

"You're very welcome. I'm just glad I was here to help." She studied me carefully. "Do you mind if I ask what happened?"

"I think you've earned that right." I paused a beat. "I'm not really sure what happened. I thought I was having hunger pains, but then I realized it was lower than my stomach. Little flutters like butterfly wings. I panicked and thought I was going into early labor. According to my book, they would never survive."

"How far along are you?" She leaned in like she was really listening to me, like she actually wanted to know and cared about what I had to say. Not like someone who was only after Grammy's money.

"Sixteen weeks," I answered.

Her entire face softened as she said with tenderness, "You were feeling your babies move for the first time."

I gasped and stared down in wonder. "That's what it feels like? Butterflies dancing in my stomach?"

She nodded slowly and lightly laughed.

I ran my hand over my silk maternity shirt. "With Matt

as the father, I figured it would feel more like a rugby team running a play when they moved."

"Just wait, dear." She patted my hand, and this time, my *heart* fluttered.

I frowned and cleared my throat. "I can't wait to tell Matt." That made me frown harder. Where had that come from, and why was I being so sentimental today? I blamed it on the hormones.

"He won't be able to feel them through your stomach just yet. Closer to twenty weeks, he should be able to." Her lips tipped up at the corners as she looked off, remembering. "Your father was in such awe the first time he felt you and your sister move."

Not enough to keep me, I thought, but remained silent.

"He actually cried." Her smile faded. "The only other time I saw him cry was when we lost you."

My heart pinched. Nope, I couldn't go there yet. I didn't know if I ever could.

"Well," I stood, "thank you again for your help. I really need to finish my grocery shopping and get back to packing."

Shoot. I squeezed my eyes closed for a second. I hadn't meant to say that part out loud, but she probably knew about my new living arrangements already anyway, given this town's rumor mill.

She stood but didn't comment on it, and her smile shined a little less brightly this time.

"You're very welcome, Tiffany. I'm always glad to help in any way I can. I mean that." Her gaze met mine and held as she spoke with sincerity. "We're not far away. Just on the edge of town in a small house on a plot of land. It's not much, but it suits us. We rarely used to come into town before, but now, well, you'll see us around a lot more." She nodded with conviction. "Your father and I are here for you if you need us, and so is your sister."

"Been there, done that. Didn't work out so well," I blurted before I could stop myself, then let out a frustrated huff.

"Give her time."

"I've given her forty years. I gave you all more than enough time. What more do you want from me?" My voice was a little harsher than I had intended.

Rita nodded, clearly unable to speak as her eyes welled up with tears. She looked like a wounded bird as she handed me a note and waved goodbye, hurrying out of the store to Charlie, who was waiting by the curb in an old, rusted pickup truck.

I sighed, feeling like the bad guy for the first time.

Dammit! Since when was any of this my fault? It hadn't been my fault before, but was it my fault now? I was a grown woman. I did have the power to make my own choices and change the course of my life if I wanted to.

It was all too much.

I opened the note. It had all of their cell phone numbers, their addresses, and said, *We love you. Please just give us a chance to make up for the past.*

Well, hell.

Chapter Thirteen

The Labor Day Bash to celebrate the end of summer turned out to be a stellar day.

Zoe had done a great job, setting up game tables, volleyball and cornhole competitions, live entertainment in the gazebo, and barbecue food trucks in the park. Vendor tents with goods for sale from the local artisans were scattered around the park.

Zoe's parents as well as her former in-laws were in town, along with Chaz's parents for the party, helping to keep an eye on her children. All seven of Harmony's brothers, along with her sisters-in-law, nieces, nephews, and parents were there, with Harmony being the only single family member. Even Homer brought a date. Morticia's father and his girlfriend were present, putting a damper on Morticia's fun.

Even though Matt and I shared a house now, we'd barely moved in and weren't even unpacked yet. We were just friends, but no one believed it, so I insisted we arrive separately for appearance's sake.

Looking around, the park was packed. This was one of Grammy's favorite parties. I felt so alone without her. Everyone else had family around, even Matt. His parents were back in Ireland still, but his uncle and cousins were here.

Rita and Charlie caught my eye. They sat up near the stage in the gazebo once more and hadn't seen me yet. I'd looked at the note she'd given me at least a hundred times, still unsure of what I wanted to do. I touched the red H pin I wore every day and renewed my resolve to be the hero of my own story.

I started to head in their direction when someone tapped me on the shoulder. Turning around, it was Tabatha. Her hair was shorter than mine but still long enough to pull into a high ponytail. She folded her hands, looking down at her sneakers for a minute, and then met my gaze with regret in her eyes.

"Hi, Tiffany," she said quietly.

"Hi, Tabatha," I responded warily.

"How are you?"

She sounded genuine, but what did I know? Clearly, I wasn't a good judge of character. I hadn't seen her or heard from her in over a month.

"I'm doing okay. Tired, but I'm not sick anymore."

"Well, that's good. Mom said you felt the babies move. That's exciting."

I folded my arms over my stomach. "What are we doing here, Tabatha?"

"What do you mean?" She couldn't quite meet my eyes.

"You haven't talked to me in five weeks, and now you're acting like we've been best friends since birth."

"I know." She wrung her hands together. "I'm sorry. I'm just nervous."

"Why?"

She finally looked me in the eye. "Because I owe you an apology."

"Okay, I'm listening..." I watched her cautiously, wondering if an unseen hammer was about to drop.

"You tried to make amends during lunch, and I shut you down. I'm sorry about that. I can be a bit hard-headed." She shrugged.

"I hadn't noticed." I laughed, losing some of my resolve. "But thank you."

She nodded. "Just because you're on Grammy's side, and I'm on Mom and Dad's, doesn't mean you and I can't meet in the middle with each other. If we're ever going to have a chance at actually being sisters, then we have to agree to disagree on who was at fault in keeping us apart. We're adults. What kind of relationship we have going forward is up to us now."

"I agree." This was an easy *yes*.

Tabatha had been wronged as much as I had, and at this stage of my life, I was cherishing the relationships I had more than ever. I was tired of the games and giving more than I got. It was time I put myself first and started demanding that the people in my life meet me halfway.

"Good. So, where do we go from here?" She looked hopeful.

"How about we try lunch again and take it one day at a time?"

"Sounds great to me." She glanced over at Rita and Charlie. "Well, I won't keep you. Enjoy the party, and I look forward to lunch soon."

"It's a date." I smiled as she walked away, feeling a seed of hope blossom.

That feeling was suffocated by weeds when I saw my ex-husband limping my way.

"Well, well, well, going solo today?" Bud looked around warily and then touched the neck brace he wore with an exaggerated grimace. "I see you don't have your bodyguard around. I knew he would get sick of you."

"A neck brace? Seriously? That's pathetic."

"You won't find it pathetic in court." He narrowed cold, dark eyes at me. "I told you this conversation wasn't over."

"You're not hurt any more than you have a bad back." I gave him a disgusted look. "You make me sick."

"And you make me greedy, you bi—"

"Easy there, laddy," came a deep rumbling voice from behind us, "I wouldn't want ye to fall again."

Bud whipped around with ease, and then immediately grabbed his neck when he realized he had an audience. "Fall?" he said loudly. "More like you pushed me."

Matt stood in a row with his cousins, Finn and Aidan, as well as what had to be his uncle, judging by the resemblance and age of him. They looked like giant sequoia trees from the redwood forest. His uncle was even bigger than he was, which I hadn't thought possible.

The tranquil grandeur of them all was awe inspiring...

And intimidating as hell.

"Pushed ye?" Matt and his crew all let out big, hearty, booming laughs. "If I pushed ye, laddy, ye wouldn't still be standing."

"That's a threat," Bud said loudly, looking around at the spectators. "I have witnesses," he added, glaring back at Matt.

Matt's grin faded into a scowl. "Ye have witnesses to what a fool ye are. I'm a lover not a fighter, but ye be testing me patience, laddy." His hands were loosely balled into fists, and his uncle cracked his knuckles, no words necessary. "I didn't so much as lay a finger on yer weak self."

"I'm not weak," Bud growled out.

"Really now?" Finn's gaze ran over the length of him.

"Hell, even I could take him," Aidan said.

"No one's going to take anyone," Matt said. "Besides, he can't prove a thing."

"Yeah? Tell it to the judge," Bud said with bravado even though his eyes were filled with worry. "You have no idea what I can do."

"Aye, but ye have no idea what we can do, and there's a whole clan of us." Matt's uncle spit to the side and clenched his jaw.

"You'll be hearing from my lawyer," Bud said, as he shuffled away.

"Shocker." I watched him go, then I turned to Matt. "Seems like you're always coming to my rescue."

"Well, if ye had let me drive us both here, then I wouldn't have to, lass."

"For the millionth time, I can take care of myself." I crossed my arms.

"I like yer lass, boy." His uncle grinned wide. "Ye've chosen well."

"Uncle Liam, this is Tiffany." Matt gave me an apologetic look. "Tiffany, this is me Uncle Liam."

Chosen? For what? My contribution to the Children of the Clover? I looked at all four of them, wondering if they all had clover tattoos. Not Aidan...yet, anyway.

I cleared my throat. "Nice to meet you, Liam, but Matt didn't choose anything," I clarified. "Because we're not anything. Well, except soon-to-be co-parents."

"Aye, whatever ye say, lass." He gestured to Finn and Aidan. "Come along, lads. Let's leave the *co-parents* to it." He led the way over to the beer tent.

"Sorry about that. The name Liam means strong-willed warrior or protector. That pretty much sums up me uncle." Matt held his hands up. "He's beyond stubborn, but there's no one I'd rather have by me side to defend me than me uncle."

"Well, that's good because I have a feeling that you're going to need to be defended." I sighed.

"I'm not worried, lass. I'm more than capable of defending meself."

"You should be. Bud is a very convincing liar." I shook my head. "I didn't tell you, but he served me with papers."

Matt's face twisted into disgust. "He's suing ye again?"

"Yes." I nodded and then felt sick over my next words. "And apparently, he's now suing you too."

"Hi, Tiffany, come on in." Victoria Steele opened the door to the Steely Knight Agency at the end of Lighthouse Lane on Freedom Lake. It wasn't too far down from Smith's Funeral Home.

"Thanks, Victoria." I took a seat at a table with plush chairs around it and a wall of windows that overlooked the lake. The sky was an ominous gray with high winds that made the lake choppy. It looked like rain at any moment.

It was a fitting day that matched my mood.

Alexandra Knight walked in with a folder. "Hi, ladies. Sorry I'm late. I was printing these images."

"What images?" I asked.

"The ones from the security camera from your salon," Alex replied.

"That's why we called you here," Vicky added.

Both women were in their fifties. Fit, fabulous and dressed to kill in power suits, with ruthless reputations. Alex had short jet-black hair that was slicked back, and deep red lipstick in sharp contrast to her pale skin. While

Vicky had buzzed platinum-blonde hair and white lipstick that stood out against her caramel skin. You could see the crafty, cunning determination blazing in both their eyes. No wonder Grammy liked them so much.

They played to win.

Alex opened the manila folder and spread the images on the table before us. Matt's back was to the camera, and he was so much bigger than Bud, it was hard to tell what had actually happened when Bud fell backwards off the porch.

Vicky hit play on her laptop, and the footage showed Matt take a quick step toward Bud, and then Bud tumbling off the porch. You couldn't see Matt's hands to tell if he pushed Bud or not, but the quick movement forward implied he did.

I squinted at the footage. "Wow, that doesn't look good."

"It's not the best look for Mr. McGinnis." Alex pursed her lips, looking thoughtful. "It's also not absolute proof that he actually laid hands on Mr. Grant."

"We need to find a way to prove he's lying about his neck injury," Vicky said.

"Easier said than done. He's good. Lying is second nature to him. He's been lying about his bad back for years. He claims I had more than enough money to support us when we were married, but I forced him to work. Since he didn't have an education, he could only get construction work, which led to a back injury."

"Is that true?" Vicky typed something into her notes.

"The back injury, yes, but not the permanent disability," I said. "When I met him, he was already a construction worker. He helped build my grandmother's house, and she knew his parents. I was blinded by his charm, but all he wanted from the start was my money. He wanted a sugar mama. He's lazy. Shortly into our marriage, he quit his job."

"How did the back injury come into play?" Alex looked up from her tablet.

"When I found out he quit his job, I threatened to leave him if he didn't go back to work. He agreed but never forgave me. His resentment turned into him downright despising me over time, and our marriage fell apart. He started cheating on me. I can handle a lot of things, but someone not wanting me is not one of them."

"What happened?" Vicky's gaze was sharp and serious.

"I served him with divorce papers, and suddenly he had an *accident*, rendering him permanently disabled." I shook my head in disgust. "He knew what he was doing. He wanted to set himself up even after our divorce so he would never have to work again. I regret the day I ever laid eyes on him."

"A judge granted him alimony?" Alex's mouth flattened into a stern line.

I nodded. "Yes. Bud claimed he didn't make enough from his disability checks to live the lifestyle he was accustomed to, and it was my fault he was in this position, so I should still have to help support him."

"And he keeps suing you for more money?" Vicky's eyes hardened.

"You got it." I like them. They were no-nonsense and tough. "Now he's upped his game because I have all of Grammy's money, and he wants more."

"Eugenia Eisenhower was one hell of a woman." Alex's jaw clenched. "We'll be damned if we'll let this scumbag take one more cent that belonged to her."

"Grammy always spoke highly of you both and appreciated you looking out for her for so many years." I was definitely happy to continue that legacy. I had used several different lawyers in the past without success. "I'm counting on you to do the same for me now."

"Oh, trust me, honey," Vicky said, with a look in her eye that meant business, "Bud Grant doesn't know who he's messing with."

Chapter Fourteen

Our ranch—it felt so weird saying *our* anything—had an open concept floor plan. When you walked through the front door into the foyer, you could see the kitchen, living room, and morning room.

The kitchen had a whole corner with two walls of white cupboards with glass doors. Marbled white, black, and taupe quartz countertops were the perfect complement. There was a gas stove, a range hood, a double-door refrigerator, and the tiled taupe backsplash set everything off perfectly.

I was in love with the island.

It was really long and had a hook on the end. It had the same marbled quartz countertop, with black cupboards beneath as an accent. The island held five bar stools and was home to a big farmhouse sink, garbage disposal, two-bin trash drawer, and dishwasher.

I loved that I could face the living room while doing

the dishes, so I would feel a part of the festivities. The living room was wide open with a stone fireplace, floating taupe mantel, and massive TV above it. Two long windows, with built-in cupboards, graced both sides of the fireplace and looked into the backyard.

My favorite room was the morning room. It was a three-walled indent off the kitchen, surrounded by windows that overlooked the backyard. So much light. I loved it. Next to it were more floating shelves above a wine bar, which wouldn't get used for a while, and a walk-in pantry.

There was a hallway on both sides of the living room, with two bedrooms on each side and two bathrooms, as well as an unfinished basement. The floor was covered with gorgeous hardwood, and we'd place area rugs in front of the massive corner couch, facing the fireplace and TV. Matt was hanging four large canvas paintings side-by-side of our beloved town of Mayflower, Massachusetts, in all four of her glorious seasons.

It was mid-September, and I was eighteen weeks. I'd been feeling the babies move more and more. The butter-flies were definitely getting stronger. Matt walked over beside me and studied his handiwork, his scent wafting to my nose, making me moan out loud.

God, he smelled amazing.

He arched a brow at me. "Was that yer stomach?"

"You know me, always hungry." For him, at the moment.

He chuckled. "That doesn't surprise me, given ye are

growing me children." He looked back at the wall. "What do ye think?" He dropped his big hands to his jeans-clad hips, which pulled his t-shirt tight across his muscles.

"I love it. I love this town, and these photos capture her in all phases of her beauty." I suddenly doubled over. "Whoa!"

His face twisted with genuine concern, melting my heart. He actually did care about these babies, and for a brief moment, I wished he cared about me as much. I shook off that foolish notion. Nothing but heartache came from wishing and dreaming.

"What's wrong?" His hands left his hips and immediately cradled both sides of my belly, sending heat radiating through me.

Speaking of phases...

The horny phase chose that moment to hit me where it counted. I pressed my lips together and struggled for control as I slowly stood up. "Nothing's wrong. It's just the twins moving again. Much stronger this time."

His eyes widened and he pressed his hands more firmly to my belly, which didn't help my situation one bit, as he waited. I tried not to squirm, allowing several moments to pass by. His shoulders drooped.

"I don't feel anything, lass."

"I'm sorry." I stepped away from his touch, for both our sakes.

"It's not yer fault." He blew out a big breath. "Ye are just lucky. I mean, I don't wish I was a woman, or anything, but a man's part in creating a baby is damn easy." He scrubbed a hand through his thick, curly, blond hair.

"And necessary." I tried to make him feel better. "I, uh, couldn't have done it without you...or at least part of you." It was a struggle to keep my eyes on his face.

"Me pleasure, lass." He chuckled. "Literally." He winked, his eyes twinkling.

I blushed, and an idea came to me. "Well, if you would like to contribute more, I could be persuaded to accommodate you..." I looked around the room. "I mean, we do live together, after all."

His gaze locked onto mine and softened. "Ye said no romance."

I shrugged. "Who said anything about romance?"

A suspicious look swam into his eyes. "Nice try." He tweaked my nose. "Ye are still not getting a look at me shamrock, if that's what yer after."

"What if I promise not to look?" I bit my bottom lip, growing desperate.

He narrowed his eyes curiously. "Does this have to do with Chapter Five?"

I blinked. "Come again?"

He nodded. "Exactly."

My jaw unhinged, and I raised an eyebrow at him. "Okay, what are we talking about?"

He laughed. "The horny phase that was in that book Zoe gave ye?"

I gaped at him. "You read my book?"

"Ye are not the only one who wants to know what to

expect during these nine months." He rubbed his hands together. "Besides, I told ye I wanted to be involved in all parts of this pregnancy."

"So, you're willing to solve my little problem then?" I fluttered my eyelashes up at him with a hopeful expression.

He laughed softly. "As much as I would love to *help* ye, I don't think being friends with benefits is a good idea, lass."

"Fine, then you'd better take the furthest bedroom down the other hallway, for both our sakes." I inhaled a long slow deep breath and held it before releasing it, as I willed myself to think of anything other than how hot he was.

The struggle was real.

He studied my flushed face. "That's probably a smart idea. And we can set up two nurseries, one down each hall-way. That way if one baby is fussy, the other won't be disturbed. And we'll take turns over who's getting up in the middle of the night." He rubbed his jaw. "Unless ye plan to breastfeed."

I was already shaking my head. "I know there is a school of thought that breast is best, and that's great for those women who choose to do so. I also know other women who physically are unable to nurse their babies, and that's okay, too. In my case, I simply don't want to, especially not two babies at the same time at my age. I think it's a personal decision that each new mother must make on her own."

"I agree, and I won't complain about getting to bottle feed me bairns." Matt nodded. "I give women so much credit. Carrying a child takes almost a year of yer life, and the changes yer body goes through are a true miracle. To nourish and develop an actual human being is remarkable. And here ye are, creating *two*. Ye are truly incredible, lass. I just wish I could feel the wee babes move."

"You and me both. I feel guilty because you can't, but Dr. Joy said you should be able to soon."

"Ah, Chapter Six." He chuckled. "I'm looking forward to it."

"And I'm looking forward to lunch." I headed to the kitchen. "What do you say we take a break and eat?"

"You got it. Grab yer coat, and I'll get my keys."

I stopped walking. "I have a better idea."

He glanced at me. "What's that?"

"I'll cook."

He halted in his tracks. "Ye cook?"

"I try," I admitted. "Zoe's been giving me lessons."

"Well, look at ye getting all domesticated."

"You can't be the only one feeding our babies." I frowned.

There was that word *our* again.

If I wasn't careful, I was going to get my heart broken without even trying.

"I'll call me mammy and get some of her recipes." Matt smiled wide. "She's an amazing cook."

"Let's not get carried away, now." I laughed. "Let's start with lunch and go from there. Deal?"

"Deal."

I WIPED my mouth with a napkin after devouring an egg salad sandwich that afternoon from the grocery store deli on my way to the mayor's office in the town hall. Let's just say the chicken salad I'd made earlier had left a bad taste in my mouth, literally. The chicken itself was overcooked and dry, and then I'd put so much mayonnaise in it, that it was more like creamy chicken soup which made the bread soggy.

I had taken one bite and then burst into tears.

Matt finished every last bite of his, but I could see the struggle on his face. Shortly after, he headed into work at the pub, probably to do the same thing I was...get some lunch that was actually edible.

I helped him clean up my failure before he headed to work and I headed to my meeting with the mayor. Walking into the town hall, I stopped short. There was Bitsy Beaumont...or Brimstone, rather.

What on earth was she doing here?

"Hi, Bitsy. Are you getting back into the party-planning business?" I took a seat in the waiting room.

"Oh, heavens no." She placed her hands on her growing belly. "Roger doesn't want me doing anything that might be taxing. He's so protective. He's going to be a wonderful father. I can just tell."

"That's great, but what are you doing *here*?" I couldn't

help blurt in frustration. I had a feeling I wasn't going to like her answer.

"Well, I know this town inside and out from all the years of my *traditional* party-planning business. I know what they want and need better than anyone. So, Mayor Edwards was all too happy to accept my help."

"Help for what exactly?" Bitsy loved to drag things out for a big reveal. It drove me crazy, not to mention, I had no patience these days.

"Why, help with all the committees, of course." She looked at me as if I were a child who needed things broken down fully to understand them. "Who better than me to know how to put all these charitable contributions to use?"

"I see." I saw what she was doing, all right.

Bitsy had to be at the heart of everything that was happening in Mayflower. She needed to feel important. To be involved. To be doing something. She had always been that way, even back in high school.

Well, not this time.

Just because she had said *yes* to Brimstone's proposal, she'd become the most respectable one of us to the town. That didn't mean she was the better person to represent my grandmother. I would be the one deciding exactly what to do with her contributions.

No one else.

"Wonderful." She smiled slowly, almost catlike. "Then you know we'll be working closely together on how best to spend your grandmother's money."

I ground my teeth and bit back what I really wanted to

say. She had some nerve. "Thank you for the offer of help, but I've got it from here."

"Oh, it wasn't an offer, darling. It's happening." She looked down her long, narrow nose at me. "I know the things that were important to your grandmother, probably better than even you do." She thrust her chin in the air and folded her hands in her lap. "It's simple. The mayor wants me on this, so I'm on it."

I set my jaw and raised my own chin even higher than hers. "Well, I don't care what Mayor—"

"Tiffany, you're here!" Mayor Edwards opened the door to his office, his face beaming with delight. "Come on in. Both of you." He nodded at Bitsy and motioned to us both. "We have lots to discuss."

Bitsy smiled pleasantly at him and gave me a smirk as she sashayed on by me like she owned the place. I followed her and bit my tongue every step of the way.

"Have a seat, ladies, have a seat." The mayor gestured towards the overstuffed white leather chairs as he closed the door behind him.

His suit was white. His desk was white. The walls, floor, and furniture...all white. He said he liked a clean slate, both personally and at work, because his wife, Eleanor, shined with enough color for the both of them.

"So, I was—" I started.

"We should do something for the school system," Bitsy cut in. "Now that I'm having a child, I understand how the parents in our community feel."

"Ah, yes, the state never provides enough funds to serve all of our children's needs." The mayor nodded.

She hadn't even given birth yet. How could she understand anything? Bitsy just had to win at all costs. Everything was and had always been a competition with Bitsy. Two could play this game.

"Grammy was big on the arts and bringing more culture to Mayflower. I know she wanted to help the local theater with renovations for a bigger stage, among other things, to help advance the program. Bring in more shows." I straightened my spine.

"That's true. Eugenia and my Eleanor loved to see those plays together." The mayor smiled fondly. "I do love the opera. Can you imagine having one right in town? Now, that's something I would take my Eleanor to."

"Our veterans could also use help with jobs and improvements to the VFW." Bitsy sat up straighter. "It's only right we provide them with what they need, after everything they've done for all of us."

"A worthy cause for sure." The mayor nodded at her.

"Grammy loved animals. She had several throughout her life. I *know* she would love to help with a bigger shelter and rescue resources. All those animals deserve a chance at a good life and finding their forever homes. Grammy would have wanted that." I stared right at Bitsy, daring her to tell me I was wrong.

She remained silent.

"Well, we have other contributors that can help fund some of these needs." He looked at me. "Ultimately,

Tiffany, you have the final say in how you wish for your grandmother's funds to be used."

"Imagine that?" I didn't even try to hide the smugness from my tone.

The mayor looked at his watch, oblivious to the game Bitsy and I had been playing. "I'd say you have lots to think about, then. I'll have my assistant draw up proposals for all of these, and you can choose which ones you want to contribute to. If that works for you, we'll go from there."

"That sounds wonderful." I stood, feeling victorious.

Until he dropped another bomb.

"And once you've made your decision, Bitsy will aid in overseeing the execution. Does that work?"

"Like a charm, Mayor. Like a charm." Bitsy looked at me. "I'll be in touch." And then she walked out the door, taking some of the thunder out of my internal victory march.

This day just kept getting better and better.

Chapter Fifteen

"Giving a sensual massage involves creating a relaxing atmosphere like the one you see here. Dim lighting, mood music, heavenly scents. Know your partner and don't use any music or scent they may not enjoy. You want to please them, not irritate them." I winked.

Jacey and Lance Winthrop were the cutest couple ever and newlyweds. They had been coming to Tiffany's Titillating Touch for regular massages separately for years. In fact, they met in the waiting room, with me playing matchmaker. Now that they were married, they wanted to learn how to give a sensual massage to each other for their honeymoon. I'd had to reschedule a couple times and so had they, but we'd finally connected.

"Are you listening, Lance?" Jacey teased.

"Oh, don't you worry. I know exactly what you like, sweetheart." Lance grinned.

"Be sure to use gentle, slow movements, focusing on each other's pleasure like I showed you both. Okay?"

They nodded.

"Always start with soft touches to warm up the body, then gradually increase pressure as desired. Pay attention to your partner's response and adjust your movements accordingly. Sound good?"

They nodded again.

"Good, because communication and consent, whether you're married or not, are key throughout the process."

"Thank you so much, Tiffany," Jacey said, her round cheeks rosy. She looked happy. "You've been amazing. This is exactly what we wanted for our honeymoon."

"It was my pleasure."

"Thank you for the recommendation of what oil to get from *Peace, Love, and Harmony*. It smells amazing and is so silky." Lance put his arm around Jacey, standing the same height as her five-foot-four frame. "I want nothing but the best for my girl."

"He's a smart man." Jacey laughed.

"You're very welcome. Harmony will see that you're taken care of. You two have a great time on your honeymoon. Be careful and take care of each other."

"Always." Jacey waved as Lance led her out of the room and down the hall toward the front.

I walked toward the back to do inventory of my supply stock. The storage room had a door that led to the back parking lot. I always kept it locked when I wasn't getting a delivery. I smelled the smoke before I saw the flames.

Oh my God...fire!

Coughing and choking on the growing smoke, I whipped open the back door at the same time that the sprinkler system and fire alarm came on. I could hear people running and screaming out of the front of the building. This wasn't just my place of business. It was my home, and, currently, Trixy's.

I stood just inside the doorway and shielded my eyes when I saw a movement in the parking lot. A woman hurried across the lot and scrambled into a car. For a moment, I thought she was a customer escaping the fire, but then I got a closer look at the driver as they sped off. There was no mistaking who it was...

Bud Grant.

Fury filled me. He was the only person who used to have a key to my home and business. I'd made him give them back after the divorce, but he'd obviously made a copy. I couldn't prove it, but I'd bet my life he'd had his latest bimbo set fire to my place.

My attorneys had been foiling his attempts at framing Matt for his so-called neck injury. That had to make him angry. but I'd never known him to be so reckless. Almost as if he were desperate, but why? I had a lot of insurance on this place. Is that what he was hoping for? My inheritance wasn't enough?

What kind of trouble had he gotten himself into this time?

Well, I had news for him. He wasn't getting one more cent from me. The wailing sirens grew closer. Someone could have been seriously hurt or died. I'd no sooner had that thought than a piece of the ceiling came crashing down, knocking me to the ground.

"Help," I called out, cradling my stomach.

My head pounded something fierce; I could barely see straight. Who was I kidding? I was sure everyone had evacuated out front, as planned. No one was in the building to hear me. I was five months pregnant, and my stomach was already growing more than average because of the twins.

The twins!

My eyes welled up with tears. What if the fall had hurt them? The ceiling had hit my head and knocked me down hard. I'd tried to protect my stomach, but it had still hit the ground fairly hard. I coughed, finding it hard to breathe even with the door open.

I was going to die never having met my babies...*our* babies.

As the world around me faded to black, all I could think about was Matt.

"Tiffany, it's Dr. Joy. Can you hear me?" She patted my cheeks.

I stirred.

"That's it. You can do it. Come back to us now." Dr. Joy had a way of being comforting yet direct. When she told you to do something, you did, no questions asked.

I stirred again, but all I wanted to do was sleep.

"Come on, lass," said a deep voice close to my ear that even in a smoke-induced coma could stir me to life. "Open those beautiful blue eyes of yers, love."

That had me blinking them open and then slamming them closed against the light. "My head." I lifted my hand and felt a bandage wrapped around my head.

"That would be the concussion you suffered." Dr. Joy spoke as she checked my vitals, and the sounds of beeping machines went off around me.

The memory of what happened came flooding back, and my hand slid to cover my stomach. "Our babies?"

"Are just fine." Matt's hand swallowed mine as he covered my stomach.

"Your sons are both doing great," Dr. Joy said.

That had my eyes blinking open wide, pain be damned. "Sons? As in both boys?" I stared up at Matt in wonder mixed with a bit of horror.

Matt's face was beaming. "Aye, lass. No wonder yer belly's so big."

I leveled a glare at him.

"I mean that in the best possible way." He cradled my cheeks and kissed my forehead. "Ye are going to be an amazing mother to these big, strapping lads."

"It's the big and strapping I'm worried about." I gestured up and down his torso. "Look at you? How am I supposed to give birth to all of that...times two?" I started to cry, terrified of giving birth. "I changed my mind. I don't want to be pregnant with your Sasquatch cubs." I was blubbering. "No, wait, I don't want to give them back.

Maybe you can have them for me. You're a legend, after all."

He shook his head, and what I could see of his eyes through my tears grew tender. "All of this didn't happen overnight," he said gently, gesturing to his torso. "Me mammy is no bigger than ye, and she did just fine. I get me size from me da's side of the family. Just look at Uncle Liam."

That only made me cry harder.

Matt looked at me with a helpless expression, at a loss for words for once.

"Get used to it." Dr. Joy patted his massive arm. "This is only the beginning. Just wait until the last trimester."

"Ah, Chapters Eighteen through Twenty." He shuddered.

"And now you passed me in the book." I sniffled. "You're the super parent. I'm the screwup. I can't even make lunch."

"Tiffany, look at me." Dr. Joy waited until I complied.

Was there ever any doubt?

I felt like I was in the principal's office...not Brimstone's. I would have rolled my eyes, but I didn't dare. Instead, I focused on Dr. Joy and listened intently to what she had to say, hoping she would restore my useless brain.

Pregnancy brain was real, and it was scary as hell because my thoughts were definitely not my own. They belonged to a mad woman who clearly needed help...if she could even remember to go to her appointment.

"Women have given birth for centuries." She patted

my hand. "Our bodies are designed for exactly that. To reproduce. It's nature's way. Freedom of choice allows us to decide whether we want to have children or not, but our bodies are ready either way."

"My body's not ready." I shook my head hard. "I worked hard for that body. It's meant for other things. Not childbirth. Definitely not childbirth. What if it fails me? I can't fail at another thing in this town. Grammy was not a failure."

A brief expression crossed the doctor's face, but it was gone before I could analyze it. "You are not your Grammy, Tiffany." She held up her hand before I could speak. "I'm not saying that's good or bad. I'm simply saying you need to stop trying to be your grandmother, and just be yourself. I, for one, think your *self* is pretty impressive."

And that was as close to a compliment anyone would ever get from Dr. Joy.

"You're right. I can do this." I inhaled a deep breath.

"Exactly. You're a woman. You can do anything. In fact, one woman in the United States alone gave birth to octuplets in California not that long ago. If she could do it, then you can definitely give birth to two babies."

"Eight babies at one time?" I looked at her in horror.

"I was just using that as an example of what is possible in nature."

"Bad example, Doc." I could feel the blood drain from my face. "They're probably like one or two pounds each. I'm going to have two babies who will probably weigh eleven pounds each. Maybe more. I mean, look at their father. What was I thinking?"

"Clearly, neither of us were, love," Matt pointed out logically.

"Not helping, Sasquatch!" I wailed.

Dr. Joy raised a brow at me, then looked at Matt, and then shrugged. "Good luck with this one."

Just then Fire Chief Wendy Monroe walked in, glanced at all of our faces, and said, "Am I interrupting something? Because I can come back."

"No!" we all yelled.

"Perfect timing, Chief." Dr. Joy grabbed her chart and stood. "I'm finished here. She's all yours." I heard her whisper, "Meet you at the pub later? You might need a drink by the time you're done."

The fire chief gave her a knowing look and nodded.

"What—" I started.

"Am I doing here?" The fire chief took the seat next to my bed on the other side of Matt. "Good question." She looked at Matt and then back to me. "Is this something you wish to discuss around other people? It pertains to your business and home."

"Former home," Matt clarified.

"I rented my apartment to my office manager, but it's still my place. My business as well," I said. "And yes, you can say whatever you need to in front of Matt. He knows all about my ex."

Matt frowned. "Yer ex?" I saw a muscle in his jaw flex. "What does he have to do with the accident at yer spa?"

Maybe this wasn't such a good idea after all.

"Oh, that was no accident," Chief Monroe said.

"How do you mean?" I refused to meet Matt's eyes because I was afraid of what I would see.

"Someone knew exactly where your security cameras were, and they disabled them. Made it look like a mechanical malfunction, but our experts could tell it was deliberately tampered with."

Bud was a former construction worker and a damn good mechanic.

"How was the fire started?" I asked.

"It was an electrical fire," the chief said. "This building is old, so the wiring is often faulty. The culprit knew that. A space heater was plugged in. It was only a matter of time before it ignited. Did you use a space heater recently?"

"Yes, when I got my last shipment of supplies in," I admitted, "but I know I unplugged it. I always do."

"That's what I thought, and given the security footage tampering, that's what raised my suspicions. Do you have a big insurance policy on this place?"

"I sure do. And my ex-husband knew all about it." My hands shook, and I clenched them into fists. "I saw a woman running away from my spa right after I discovered the fire. I thought she was a customer fleeing, but then I noticed she jumped into a car. I saw the driver's face as they sped off."

"And who did you see?" she asked.

"Bud Grant." I dared to look at Matt's face.

If he wasn't the father of my babies, I would be scared as hell right now.

Chapter Sixteen

Two weeks later, we were at a girls' night at Morticia's house. Her apartment had white walls with black furniture and accent pieces. Tonight's snacks were properly displayed tapas on classic dove-gray plates. She didn't have color anywhere, which made the brightly colored foods even more appetizing. We'd tried to add a bit of color to her life with gifts, but then we stopped trying to make her into something she wasn't. She enjoyed a simple, minimalist pallet.

And books, of course.

Books were everywhere. Her free time was spent with us, or reading, or in her online book clubs. For once, I was the first one there. I picked up a half-read copy of Oliver King's latest thriller.

"Don't lose my place!" she hollered from the kitchen.

I carefully set the book down. "No worries, doll. I've got your back."

"I have book club online later tonight, and we're discussing that book. There's this guy in my online group, Collin Quin, who drives me crazy. He acts like he knows Oliver King better than I do." She snorted. "Not likely. I am most definitely his biggest fan, and I intend to prove that tonight."

Zoe walked in. "Hey, ladies, sorry I'm late. Mrs. Bee took forever to come over to watch the kids. Chaz got called in to perform an emergency C-section on one of his expectant mothers." She glanced at me. "Sorry, hon. Didn't mean to scare you."

"I'm not scared," I lied, but even I had felt the blood drain from my face.

Harmony came barreling through the door. "Pour me a beer, babe. I'm finally here, and I could definitely use a drink."

"Here you go." Morti handed her a tall one.

"Why, what's wrong?" Zoe asked, as Morti handed her a glass of chardonnay and took the seat beside her.

I joined them at the kitchen table and sat in front of the bottle of sparkling water Morti had placed at my setting.

"What's wrong?" Harm snorted as she plopped down beside me and drained half the pint. "My mother, that's what. She used to set me up on blind dates all the time, but they never worked out. It drove me crazy, so I told her to stop, and she did."

"And that's wrong how...?" Morti arched a jet-black eyebrow high.

"She picks *now* to start listening to me?" Harm huffed out a breath. "If I don't get laid soon, I'm going to explode."

Zoe spit her chardonnay all over the table. "Oh, I'm so sorry, Morti." She dabbed at the table with a napkin.

"You're fine. At least you don't drink red wine." Morti got up to grab more towels, black of course.

"I'm just so frustrated with her. She's either pimping me out or telling me I'm acting like a hooker." Harm threw her hands up. "Then she got mad when I corrected her and said like a slut, not a hooker, because I was willing to give it away for free."

"Good lord, doll, you're going to give your mother a heart attack." I nibbled on some cheese from the gorgeous charcuterie board filled with a selection of cured meats, an assortment of cheeses, crackers and bread, olives and pickles, fruit, nuts, dips and spreads. Morti had done a great job.

"All I know is that none of the decent men in town will even give me a chance. I'm getting desperate enough to give it a try with one of the freakshows she tries to fix me up with, but now she's put the kibosh on that. First, she thinks I don't like men, and now she thinks I'm a nymphomaniac. I can't win. Mayflower is a small town. At this point, the men in town just flat-out think I'm crazy. Am I really that scary?"

We all hesitated.

"Don't answer that." Harm downed the rest of her beer.

"You're not crazy," I said gently, "you're just misunderstood."

"Aren't we all." Morti grunted.

"You just haven't found the right man, hon," Zoe added. "When you do, you'll know it. He'll love you for you and all of your quirks, just like we do."

"That's right, girl." Morti raised a glass of diet cola. "To Harmony Jones. You're the best." She clinked her glass with all of ours.

"Thanks, babes. You girls are awesome. I seriously couldn't do any of this without you, nor would I want to."

"I'd drink to that if I could," I said, then sipped my water.

"So, how are you doing, really?" Zoe looked at me with concern. "Chaz has been keeping me updated on your concussion."

"I'm getting better every day, and the Sasquatch cubs are fine." I patted my twenty-two-week belly. "Thanks for asking, doll."

"What about your spa?" Harmony scowled. "I hope Matt found the dipshit and ripped him a new shamrock."

"You and me both, but unfortunately, Bud knows how to hide when he wants to." I sighed. "Thankfully the fire department put the fire out rather quickly. Only my supply room and supplies were damaged from the fire and smoke. The rest of the place had water damage, but that's all being fixed as we speak."

"Does it affect your bottom line?" Morticia took a sip of diet cola.

"I had to move everyone's appointments out a month, and Trixy is dealing with the water damage upstairs in the apartment, but she's been very understanding. Obviously, I won't charge her rent until it's fixed."

"I just don't get why Bud would do something like that?" Zoe shook her head as she popped an olive into her mouth, looking off pensively. "He's already suing you for more alimony because of your grandmother's inheritance. What's the purpose of trying to burn your place of business down?"

"To get back at her for having such kick-ass lawyers." Harm chugged her second beer straight from the bottle then set it on the table, making a loud clunk.

"Or to collect on the insurance money." Morti eyed Harm with brows drawn together in disapproval, then slid a coaster in her direction.

"Or just to be an ass," I admitted. "The man is not happy unless he wins, and he hasn't won yet. His ego can't handle being a constant loser. Ladies, Bud has succeeded in getting on the one nerve I have left. I need to find a way to prove he's been faking everything for years. He's taking things too far, and someone could have gotten seriously hurt."

"*You* got seriously hurt," Zoe pointed out. "Not to mention, now he's hurting you financially."

"How's Matt taking it all?" Harm tilted her head and studied me.

"Not well." I shook my head slowly, looking around the

table until I met each of their eyes. "I'm afraid he's going to do something he might regret."

"Like what?" Morti wrinkled her brow.

"I honestly don't know." Memories of the look he had given when he found out Bud was behind the fire flooded my mind. "You should have seen his face. It was downright scary." I rubbed my arms. "We live together, but I've barely seen him. He hasn't been around much in the past two weeks."

"What do you think he's been doing?" Zoe grabbed a throw from the couch and draped it around my shoulders.

"Thanks." I smiled at her, but then my smile slipped as I thought about her question. "All I know is Matt said he was going to make Bud stop harassing me, once and for all. What if he gets arrested? I admit I've dated bad boys before, but I've never had children with them. I can't have my baby daddy behind bars."

"Matt's a smart guy." Harm lifted one shoulder. "Family means too much to him. Not just his sons, but his uncle and the family who work for him. He's not going to let them down by getting arrested."

"I sure hope not." I thought about her words. "Speaking of sons, I still can't believe I'm having two boys. Do you know what that means?"

"That you're worried they'll be huge like their daddy?" Morticia asked.

"Yes, there is that, but that's not my biggest worry."

"If you're worried they'll be wild and crazy, the answer is *they will*. I have two," Zoe said, adding, "but with girls come tears and drama. It all evens out in the end. You'll be fine. In fact, I think you'll surprise yourself and be a wonderful mother."

"Thank you for that, but that's not it, either."

Harmony's eyes twinkled. "You're worried they'll be recruited as Children of the Clover."

"Exactly!" I said. "I have to up my game if I'm ever going to rest easy. I need to know once and for all if the legend is true. Did Matt tattoo his penis with a four-leaf clover because of a stupid cult, and will he try to make his boys follow in his footsteps?"

"I really do think you're being paranoid and overreacting because of some silly book," Zoe said.

"Silly or not," I said with determination, "no one is laying a finger on *any* part of my babies if I have anything to say about it."

Late that evening, I heard Matt come home.

It was becoming less and less strange to consider the ranch that Matt and I shared as home. We'd been living together for six weeks now. It felt like a lot longer than that, especially when he had been glued to my side right up until the past two weeks. Of course, he still made sure I was eating right and taking my vitamins. He either cooked or brought food home before I even had a chance to try making another meal.

But I still hadn't given up on my lessons from Zoe.

I rolled out of bed...yes *rolled*, because it was getting more and more difficult to use my core. I had to pee constantly during the middle of the night. I used the master bathroom which was attached to my bedroom in my hallway of the house. One other bedroom was in this hallway. Then Matt's hallway had two bedrooms and a full bath.

After I was finished, I didn't go back to bed. I crept down the hall until I reached the living room. Matt had gone down his hallway. I could hear the shower come on in his bathroom and folk music come on. Inspiration struck. Grabbing cleaning supplies from the walk-in pantry, I made my way down his hallway and prayed he hadn't locked the door.

He hadn't.

It was my lucky day, and I was hoping I was lucky enough to see that damned fourth leaf. I quietly opened the door, but the room was filled with steam. Who knew Matthew McGinnis liked a long, hot shower? I would have to tell him that hot water wasn't good for his skin. I shook my head to focus.

Holding my cleaning spray in one hand, I squirted the glass shower door and began to wipe, straining to see anything. Darnit! The steam was on the inside of the glass door. His hip suddenly brushed the glass, wiping a section clear. A flesh-colored image began to emerge, and I held my breath, squinting, then blew out a big puff of air almost immediately.

Another side-effect of turning forty...

I suddenly needed glasses.

Double Darnit!

I started rubbing harder, when the shower door flew open, blasting me in the face with steam and water. I shrieked and fell forward, grabbing onto him around the waist.

"Tiffany?" he sputtered.

"In the flesh," I said, then corrected, "er, at least you are, I mean." Even if I pulled away, I wouldn't be able to see the fourth leaf unless he grew hard.

Wonder of wonders, I felt a stirring against my chest.

I bit my bottom lip and started to lean back, but in the time it took me to blink the water from my eyes, Matt had whisked me into his arms and marched me out of the bathroom. Buck naked and dripping wet, he barreled down the hall, through the living room, down my hall, and into my bedroom.

Good thing it was the middle of the night, or he might have scared the neighbors through our curtainless living room windows. He could have given poor Mrs. Cartright a heart attack...or palpitations of another kind. Speaking of palpitations, of course, the lights were out in my room.

Darnit!

I could see his shadow looming over me. His fully erect shadow. Damn, my mouth watered. He was one impressive, godlike man, even in the dark. I could understand why women would want him to spread his seed.

He was magnificent!

"Holy Mary Mother of God, what in the name of Saint

Monica be ye doing in me bathroom?" he finally spoke, apparently praying for Monica's patience.

"Sorry, um, I was sleepwalking?" I laughed nervously over my question-like response. "I think they call it nesting."

"Chapter Eighteen." He nodded, inhaling a few deep breaths. "I think it best if ye clean yer own nest next time, preferably in nighties that aren't see-through, or I can't be held accountable fer what might happen."

"What if I want to nest in your bed?" I bit my bottom lip hopefully. "I mean, not like birds that mate for life, or anything. I just want to mate." I laughed over how ridiculous I sounded even to my own ears. "Second trimester still, remember?"

"Aye, how in the hell could I forget?" He scrubbed a hand over his wet hair. "Not tonight, love," he said firmly, obviously in no mood for games. "Not tonight. It's been a helluva couple of weeks. All I want is to sleep for a week. Can ye grant me that, lass?"

"Only if ye come clean with me over what yer about on the morrow, savvy?" I blinked. Sleep deprivation and its effect on the brain was no joke.

"What accent, pray tell, is that?"

"An Irish pirate?" I laughed. "I have no clue. But what I do know is that you've been keeping something from me for a couple of weeks now. Where have you been going?"

"I'll fill ye in on everything, I promise. In the meantime, take care of me bairns and get some sleep...*savvy?*" I could just make out his smile.

"Deal."

He leaned down like he always did when he kissed me on the forehead. Only, this time his lips landed on mine, and I forgot to breathe. He didn't touch me anywhere else. Just his full lips moving sensually over my mouth, but then he slipped his thick tongue inside to dance with mine.

Stars swam behind my eyes, and liquid heat pooled between my legs.

He tasted like Guinness, thyme, and bay leaves, with a touch of something uniquely Matt. I was drowning and loving every minute of it. Who was I fooling? I didn't want to just mate. I wanted this man to *be* my mate, but that scared the hell out of me. I had to have been giving him so many mixed signals.

We'd done everything backwards.

He pulled slowly away, his shadow more magnificently erect than ever. "Goodnight, love."

I swallowed hard, unable to speak. All I knew for certain was that I was in a whole lot of trouble.

Chapter Seventeen

The next morning—late morning—Matt finally woke up. He walked into the kitchen, scrubbing a hand through his hair, his eyes still a little puffy from sleep. "Wow, I slept like the dead. Everything is a blur."

I paused a beat. "Everything?"

His gaze met mine. "Well, not everything, love." He winked.

"About that," I stared him down and pointed a wooden spoon at him. "What about the no-romance agreement?"

"I could ask ye the same thing. Ye jumped me in the shower in the middle of the night..." he leaned forward, "... while I was *naked*."

"I was nesting, remember?" I blinked rapidly and felt a bead of sweat trickle down between my breasts.

His gaze heated as he followed its path, his voice growing husky. "I remember ye wanted to nest in me bed."

"So, are you hungry?" I blurted, desperate to change the subject.

His lips formed a slow, sexy smile. "I'm starved, love."

My face flamed red. "Er, for food, I mean. I cooked." I pointed at the pile of scrambled eggs. "It might not look pretty, but I tried a bite, and I think it's actually edible."

"Thanks. I haven't had an actual meal in weeks." He sat down at the table as if that dangerously delicious conversation hadn't just happened and dug into the plate of eggs, toast, and bacon. "This is great, lass."

Damn stage two.

Maybe my active imagination was making me read into things. I shook off my wayward thoughts and focused on the real reason I'd made him breakfast. I cleared my throat before responding.

"You're welcome." I sat down next to him, having already eaten mine because I couldn't wait. "So, why exactly haven't you had a meal in weeks?" He'd promised to come clean the next day, and that day was today.

His gaze met mine. He didn't speak until he finished chewing and wiped his mouth. He took a sip of orange juice, as if stalling to find the right words. Letting out a big sigh, he finally said, "I've been following yer ex."

"Bud?"

Matt arched a thick blond brow high. "How many exes do ye have?"

I narrowed my eyes. "Very funny...not. Mind telling me why you were following my ex-husband?"

He hoisted one massive shoulder. "To make him stop harassing ye."

I threw up my hands. "If you get into a fight with him, he's going to sue you. The last thing I need is for the father of my children to get arrested."

Matt waved me off. "Ye worry too much, lass. The only one who's getting arrested is that lying fake."

I frowned. "What do you mean?"

"I did a little research. Found out where he lives." He held up his hand. "Not so I could go beat him up, even though he deserves it. I went to his house to stake it out." Matt's face hardened. "Just as ye suspected, he's been faking everything."

"I knew it!" I slapped my palm on the table. It felt great to be right and actually have someone believe me. "Do you have proof?"

"Not yet. But I did see him with me own two eyes. He wasn't wearing a neck brace, and for someone with a bad back who can't work, he looked pretty limber to me climbing a tree. It looked like he was getting a cat down for some woman."

Disgust filled me. "Probably his new girlfriend. The one I saw running to his car the day my spa was set on fire."

"I wasn't prepared the first day and my pictures all came out blurry." Matt set his jaw. "I've been back every day since, following him all over town, waiting for him to slip up again."

"Good." My face matched his.

He blinked. "Ye approve?"

"As long as you don't do anything to get arrested, then yes. I'm tired of fighting this battle alone and getting nowhere." My shoulders drooped. "I just don't have the energy anymore."

"I've got enough energy for the both of us, love. Ye leave the weasel to me." He stood up and carried his dishes to the kitchen sink.

I walked over to refill my teacup, not expecting him to turn around at that moment. We collided, and his arms instantly wrapped around me to steady me. Our bodies were pressed together, and I sucked in a breath, surprised.

"Easy, love." He looked down at me but didn't move away. "Yer carrying precious cargo." His eyes sprang wide. "What was that?"

I was twenty-two weeks, but the timing had never been right until now. "That was your precious cargo telling you you're squishing them, Daddy."

His entire face filled with wonder and then melted. He slid his hands down my arms, pausing just before touching my belly. "May I?"

I laughed softly. He'd touched every inch of me not that long ago, yet this somehow felt far more intimate. "Of course."

His huge palms cradled both sides of my rounded stomach, and I could feel the comforting warmth. I felt a foot kick, possibly more than one foot, and I gasped. "That was a big one."

"Aye, strong and full of life. This is incredible," he said in barely more than a whisper, his face one big beaming smile with perfect white teeth. He looked up from my belly with moisture shining in his sparkling blue eyes. "Ye are incredible."

"And you're going to make me cry." I laughed past the lump in my throat as I stepped away to refill my teacup to go. He was an open book. At any given moment, you knew what Matthew McGinnis was thinking. He didn't hide his feelings and wasn't afraid to be vulnerable. I envied that. What it must be like to be so carefree.

"Ye don't take compliments very well, do ye," he said quietly.

I startled for a moment, realizing he must have read *my* face for a change. "Trust me, doll, I'm used to compliments." I brushed him off like it was no big deal, sliding my mask back into place.

"I'm sure ye are. Ye are a beautiful woman, love." His tone filled with tenderness. "I'm talking about yer inner beauty. You're glowing, lass. Motherhood suits ye. And I know ye don't think ye'll be any good at it, but ye already are. Ye just need to believe it like I do. So, I repeat...ye are incredible."

"And late." I inhaled a shaky breath and pasted on a smile. "I should probably head to work."

It didn't matter how many rules we set in place. He saw through my bullshit, straight to my vulnerable soul. Damnit! How had I let this happen? I was falling hard, and it scared the hell out of me. No more trying to check out his clover tattoo. It was too risky. I had to pull back. Put some distance between us...

Before I suffered a loss I couldn't recover from.

With that thought, I grabbed my bag and headed out the door before I did something stupid, like fall in love with him.

OVER THE NEXT TWO WEEKS, I did my best to do exactly that, but it was pointless. Matt was more present than ever. He hired a private investigator to tail Bud and gave his cousin Aidan more duties at the bar while Finn kept an eye on everything as he performed. That freed up Matt's time to spend with me.

I got used to having him around.

He hadn't brought up romance or vulnerability or anything that made me uncomfortable. It was as if he knew I might bail if things got to be too much. Instead, he acted like a perfect gentleman. A housemate. A friend. He cooked and cleaned and contributed just as much as I did. We decorated both nurseries, as well as the rest of our ranch together.

The babies had made it to twenty-four weeks gestation. That was considered severely premature, but there was a chance they could survive at that age if I went into premature labor. A big sigh of relief for us both. Twins were usually born early, but I was hoping to make it as long as possible.

Our vehicles both had car seats installed and double strollers loaded in the trunks. He'd even packed a diaper bag with outfits to go home in, as well as newborn diapers, wet wipes, burp cloths, pacifiers, and even toys. He'd thought of everything, even me, but I refused to let him pack my bag, but he had inspired me to do so myself. Zoe was right. My clothes were definitely comfy these days, but...

No one was getting a look at my granny preggo panties.

I glanced at my watch. Where were they?

I sat at a table in Lolita's Restaurant, waiting for Tabatha and Rita to join me. My sister and I had lunch once before alone, with a new understanding and appreciation for each other and the unusual circumstances that had torn us apart and now brought us back together. It had gone well, so we decided to do it once more.

Only this time, she'd talked me into letting Rita join us.

"Sorry we're late," Tabatha said, as they approached my table.

I jumped because I hadn't seen them coming. "It's okay," I said, because I couldn't think of anything else to say. I glanced at Rita, who looked like a wounded bird again, and I still felt uncomfortable.

"Yes, sorry." Rita smiled tentatively, staring intensely at me as if terrified of what my reaction would be.

"It's my fault," Tabatha interjected. "My meeting with an author I'm working with took longer than I expected."

I smiled at them both. "Really, it's okay. Why don't you both have a seat."

Rita let out the breath she'd been holding and practically wilted into the chair across from me, while Tabatha sat confidently in the chair next to me. Clearly, we didn't get our gumption from Mommy Dearest.

That was all Grammy.

The corner of my lip tipped up, thinking of her.

It had been four months since her death. I'd had all of her personal belongings brought to a storage unit and sold her house with the furniture in it, but I still couldn't go through her things. I had my own money, so I set up a trust fund for the boys.

I still cried myself to sleep many nights, and I missed her terribly. That's what made this so hard. I didn't want to hear anything negative said about the woman I adored. She was tough, but she had always been fair and kind to me. She loved me, and she was mine. She wasn't perfect, but who was?

I couldn't risk anyone ruining her memory for me.

"Tiffany, did you hear me?" Tabatha eyed me curiously.

I blinked. "Sorry, I was lost in my thoughts."

"Good ones, I hope." Rita looked over the top of her menu at me.

I sat up a little straighter. "Yes, they were of Grammy."

"Ah, Eugenia was a remarkable woman," she said softly, her eyes filled with kindness and regret.

"She certainly was." I couldn't help liking Rita and wanting some kind of relationship with her, but I felt guilty, like I was betraying Grammy. So, I settled on being cordial to Rita and focusing on developing my relationship with Tabatha.

The waitress came over and we ordered. After she left, someone else brought our drinks right away, and we waited in awkward silence for our food.

"Dad told me to tell you he noticed an oil stain beneath your car." Tabatha took a sip of lemonade. "He can help you with that if you'd like. He's pretty handy with cars."

"Oh, yes, your father restores old cars on the side when he's not working for the brewery. He's quite good." Rita beamed with pride.

"I don't need Charlie's help. I have Matt."

Rita's shoulders slumped and she toyed with her napkin. "I'm glad you have someone to help you, dear."

I nodded, unable to speak. How could a simple term of endearment like the word *dear* from a person's biological mother stir up so many emotions. As I did with everything these days, I blamed the hormones.

"How are you feeling?" Tabatha glanced at my stomach and smiled, but I could see the pain she still felt over losing her daughter and husband shining bright in her eyes like my own. Like our mother's.

Maybe this lunch wasn't such a great idea after all.

I inhaled a deep breath, reminding myself I was an Eisenhower. I could do this. "I feel great. I'm nearing the end of my second trimester. The first trimester was awful. I was so tired and sick. But the second trimester has been much better so far. I feel great. It fills my mind with wonder to feel the boys move. Carrying twins isn't so bad."

Tabatha snorted. "I'll remind you of that during the third trimester."

I frowned. "Why?"

"Tabatha, don't scare your sister. It's nothing she can't handle." Rita sat up straighter and seemed less wilted as she turned to me. "You'll be just fine, Tiffany."

"What aren't you telling me?" I stared wide-eyed at my mother and then looked at my sister. "Seriously, I want to know what to expect."

"Don't you have a book?" Tabatha shrugged at Rita when she scowled at her.

"Yes, but I have a feeling it leaves out the details an expectant mother really wants to know. So, fess up, Tabby. What was it *really* like for you?"

"Sorry, Mom, Tiff asked for it. And honestly, I would have been better prepared had you told me what it was really like."

"Every woman is different, and I just don't believe in unnecessarily scaring a pregnant woman when she can't reverse what's going to happen." She sat back and folded her hands as our food arrived, as if she were at a tea party and they hadn't just terrified me.

It felt like forever until the waiter finally left. They both started eating, but suddenly, my appetite was gone. "Um, excuse me, sister," I clutched her arm, "but talk and eat at the same time please. Because I can't eat a bite until I know what I'm in for. And don't sugarcoat it. I'm an Eisenhower, remember? I can take it."

She sighed and put her hamburger down. "I only carried one baby, but I can tell you your cute little belly won't be so cute anymore. You won't be able to see your feet or tie your own shoes. You'll have to pee constantly, and don't be surprised if you wet your pants a time or two. Your back will ache from standing with a permanent arch. You'll be starving, but you won't have any room in your stomach, so you'll want to eat all day long."

I felt my skin pale as the blood drained away from my face.

"And don't get me started on the heartburn. The kicks will feel like an MMA fight is happening and your uterus is the arena, with a foot or two getting stuck beneath your ribs. Then there are the stretchmarks on your breasts, belly, and thighs no matter how much fancy cream you rub on them. With twins, expect double the amount."

Little stars danced before my eyes, and my head grew light and spacey.

"Then there are the Braxton Hicks contractions. You'll think you're in actual labor, but you're not. It's only the warmup and nothing like the main event. My labor lasted three days, and I was too late for pain meds..."

Her words faded as the darkness closed in, and the lights went out in Mayflower, leaving me with one final thought...maybe Eisenhowers weren't as tough as I thought they were.

And then I had no thoughts at all.

Chapter Eighteen

"I can't believe I fainted." I placed two adorable, light-up ceramic pumpkins in my shopping cart the next day.

"Chaz said stress can really take a toll on a person's body, especially a pregnant woman, and you're not just any pregnant woman. You're having twins. Make sure you take it easy." Zoe tossed a bunch of cobwebs in her basket.

Zoe had a Halloween party she was planning for the Wellingtons. They were friends of my grandmother, and their son was the man Grammy had wanted me to marry. Instead, I'd married her other friend's son, Bud Grant. He'd been handsome and charming, while Nelson Wellington had been stuffy and boring.

Turns out Grammy knew best.

Stuffy and boring was loyal and still married.

"How cool is this?" Harm snagged a red-headed witch that looked surprisingly life-like to put by her front door.

Her eyes were drawn to a man down the aisle headed our way. "Hey, there, Peter Sherman. Haven't seen you in forever, my dude. How's it hangin', bro?" She grinned and waggled her eyebrows.

His eyes widened, and then he quickly turned around and walked the other way.

"See what I mean? I can't even get Pewee Sherman to talk to me." She blew out a frustrated breath. "A few months ago, he had been begging my mother to set us up on a date. I don't get it." She sniffed her shirt. "Do I smell?"

"You smell great with all the amazing products in your shop. But, um, is that the way you always talk to guys?" Morti wrinkled her nose.

Harm shrugged. "What's wrong with the way I talk?"

"Nothing when you talk to us, hon," Zoe pointed out gently, "but, well, you might want to try sounding less like your brothers when you talk to men."

"And the eye wagging might be a bit too much, doll." I patted her arm.

"Really?" Harm sighed. "I guess my desperation is starting to show. Thanks for keeping it real, babes. I need all the help I can get in the romance department."

"You know we're here for you." Morticia graced Harmony with a rare smile, then her eyes lit up when she spotted a full skeleton and immediately put it in her cart.

"Great costume," a man said as he walked by Morti.

"Oh, it's not a costume." She pointed at the heap of bones doubled over. "He's a skeleton."

"Huh?" the man said, just now noticing the skeleton in

her cart, then scratched his head. "I meant your whole getup. The outfit and wig."

"Well, that's not a costume either. So, there's that." Morti shrugged. She'd left her long black hair down for once and was wearing her usual black attire but this time a dress since she had a funeral to help conduct later.

The man flushed a red the color of beets then grabbed his *silent* phone and held it to his ear. "What's that? Of course. I'll be right there." He slid his phone back into his coat pocket. "Gotta go meet the wife at the butcher." He left his half-full cart in the middle of the aisle and made a beeline for the door.

Morti shook her head and looked at Harm. "You think you've got problems. Try being me for a day."

"You're both gorgeous, intelligent, funny, amazing women. If any man can't see that, then he's not worthy of either of you. There's someone out there for you both. I just know it." I patted my growing tummy. "Meanwhile, I'm a mess. Tabatha was right. This morning, I couldn't tie my own shoes. That set me off on a thirty-minute crying tangent. Then Matt slipped these fuzzy slippers with thick arch-supported soles on my feet."

"I have to admit I never thought I'd see the day Tiffanie Eisenhower wore fuzzy slippers in public." Zoe winked at me as she loaded her cart with several strings of spider lights with glowing orange eyes.

"They are the most comfortable shoes. It's like walking on clouds." I shook my head. "My whole world has changed. I used to care so much about how I looked. Now, it's all about the comfort."

"Amen to that." Morti tossed a couple tombstones into her basket.

"So, how did it go with your sister and mother, Tiff?" Harm grabbed a broomstick and cauldron, adding them to her cart.

"Awkward," I admitted. "Tabatha and I are progressing. We've met a couple times for lunch and even exchanged text messages a few times." I lifted my hands, palms up. "It's Rita. I know she's trying, but it's just weird. She really doesn't act anything like how Grammy made her out to be. She seems genuine, and that confuses me."

"Don't stress, hon." Zoe gave me a hug.

"I just feel so guilty because I actually like her." I wiped away a tear. "I never heard Grammy say a single nice thing about Rita. I could tell she cared about her, but she was angry and hurt and about as stubborn as they came. I'm afraid she's rolling over in her grave at me talking to my own mother. And I have to admit...I like having a sister. I know I have you ladies, and you know you're my soul sisters, but to have an actual blood sister is special. I never believed in the twin thing, but there is something about her that draws me in."

"It's okay to do what you want to, Tiff." Morti squeezed my hand. "Your grandmother would want you to be happy."

"She's right." Zoe nodded.

"I don't believe it!" Harm ran over to a bin.

We all jumped.

"Don't believe what?" I shuffled over to join her with Zoe and Morti hot on my fuzzy heels. There was a bin full of pumpkins, leprechauns, and pots of fake gold. Then my gaze zoomed onto the item Harm held in her hand, and I gasped.

A string of four-leaf clover lights.

I met each of their eyes. "It's a sign."

"You're not still entertaining the idea that Matt is a member of the Children of the Clover cult, are you?" Zoe groaned.

"Signs don't lie. Right, Harm?" I looked at her with raised eyebrows.

"She does have a point." Harmony lifted one shoulder. "There have been a lot of signs lately that point to clovers."

"It's not a sign. It's a store that sells old merchandise. I'm with Zoe on this one, Tiff." Morticia stared at me with a serious expression filled with worry. "You've got a good thing going with Matt. Careful about taking this whole clover tattoo thing too far. It just might blow up in your face."

"That's okay by me." I added every strand of the clover lights to my cart and headed for the register as I called over my shoulder, "Then I can get a good look and put this legend to bed once and for all."

Matt got a good chuckle over my clover lights and adored my little light-up pumpkins. I'd even worn a big pumpkin-colored sweatshirt that said *Mama Pumpkin*, with a cute little green stem hat and green maternity leggings, with my fuzzy slippers, of course. While Matt wore a *Pumpkins are my Jam* t-shirt that hugged every muscle, leaving nothing to the imagination, with a pair of jeans that hugged his buns and thighs.

Let's just say it had been really difficult to focus on the children.

We'd handed out candy and even shared some apple cider with our neighbor, Mrs. Cartright. She was a widow, whose children and grandchildren all lived away, so she adored us and our growing family.

During the next two weeks, no matter how close I tried to get to Matt, nothing "blew up." Not his ego. Not his libido. Not his temper. Nothing. He was onto me and now locked both his bedroom and bathroom doors.

We'd fallen into a routine of sorts, living life and co-existing in the same house as if we were a real couple. A family. Except for the no-romance rule. Matt wasn't my lover, but he didn't feel like a friend, either.

He felt like something more.

I knew he liked most foods but hated pickles and creamed corn. His favorite color was green—go figure—and he loved reading. His favorite sport was hockey. He was afraid of heights and spiders. He rarely got angry, but when he did, you'd best not be on the receiving end. He was fiercely loyal and protected what was his. Yet he got teary-eyed over sappy greeting cards, and that endeared him to me even more.

He was a big teddy bear on the inside.

He discovered I loved French food, wasn't big on vegetables, and loved bread. I didn't really care about sports. I liked to read, but loved a good drama or romantic comedy movie. I loved to travel and was into art. I had a fear of drowning and hated rodents of any kind. I was also very loyal to my small circle and would defend them to the end.

Our conversations had started getting deeper lately.

"So, I know you have a big family, but I don't know much else about them." I was leaning back on our massive couch with my feet up on an ottoman.

Matt was giving me a foot rub while I sipped hot chocolate. I was twenty-six weeks and feeling enormous. It was mid-November now and chilly, so he had turned the fireplace on. His hands were huge, and I couldn't help moaning. He gave the best foot massages. The human foot had so many nerves in it. Carrying around all this extra weight made my feet ache something fierce, and what his hands were doing to them was literally orgasmic.

His lips tipped up at the corners over my moans of pleasure as he switched to my other foot and began to speak. "Well, I am the middle child of five. Two older brothers who help me dad run the family pub in Ireland. And two younger sisters who help me mam run her catering business."

"How come you moved to Mayflower?" My entire

body felt so relaxed and cozy as I took another sip of hot chocolate.

"Me uncle wanted to train me to take over his pub, and I wanted an adventure." He finished with my other foot and moved onto my calves.

"Do you have any regrets?" My eyelids grew heavy.

His gaze held mine captive. "Not a one, love. Not a one." He paused a minute to study me. "Do ye?"

"Do I what?" I was half out of it.

"Have regrets."

"Several," I admitted. I tended to be more guarded than him, so when that came out of my mouth, I blinked.

He frowned. "I see."

I was already shaking my head. "No, you don't. My regrets aren't about you. I might not have planned to have children, but now that I'm pregnant, I can't imagine the idea of not having them in my future."

He relaxed and covered my feet with the blanket then joined me on the couch, resting his feet on the ottoman as well. Our bodies touched from our shoulders to our feet. It felt natural to tip my head until it rested on his shoulder.

"What are yer regrets, then?" He leaned his head down to rest on the top of mine as I talked.

I opened up about my ex, and everything else spilled out. I told him about my grandmother, my parents, and my sister. My fears about giving birth and being a bad mother. Guilt about wanting a relationship with my birth mother. Betraying Grammy. Worrying about living up to her reputation and how to do her proud.

"Mostly, I regret ever letting myself be vulnerable," I said softly.

"Letting down yer walls and being vulnerable is a good thing, lass," his deep voice rumbled close to my ear.

"Not for me."

"And why's that?" His voice was filled with compassion.

I swallowed the lump in my throat. "Because I get hurt every single time."

"How so?"

"Every time I let someone in, they reject me. It makes me feel like I'm not enough. I wasn't enough at birth for my parents to keep me. I wasn't enough for my husband to stay faithful to me. I'm not enough for this town to respect me." My voice grew even more emotional. "And I wasn't enough for your family to approve of me."

"Hey, now." He tilted my face up until I looked at him. "That's not true, love. That was me fault."

"It was?" I was mesmerized by his eyes.

"Aye." He nodded slowly. "I fancied ye."

"Y-You did?" I would have believed anything he said to me at this moment.

"Yes, but ye made it clear ye didn't fancy me back."

I blinked. "That's definitely not true." I thought he knew how I felt about him, but then I realized I'd never actually said the words.

"Okay, so ye lusted after me, but that was it. I wanted more than just a one-night stand. I wanted it all." His gaze traced the features of my face. "I wanted it with ye." He was so close I could feel his breath on my cheeks.

I swallowed hard. "Then why did you say I wasn't the type of woman you would bring home to your mammy because I am divorced?"

"I was angry because I thought ye only wanted to prove some stupid legend, and I didn't want to start something that would only end up with me getting hurt." He sighed. "Ye made it clear you never wanted to get married again or have children."

"Well, I'm having children now." I laughed.

He shook his head. "Aye, and ye still don't want romance."

I sat up a little straighter. "Because I don't want to get hurt again."

He nodded. "I know, lass, but where does that leave us?"

All my bravado left my body on a big exhale. "I honestly don't know."

"I'm not yer ex, love, and I would never hurt ye." His eyes looked sad, and all I wanted to do was make his pain go away.

"Matthew..." His name was a whisper on my lips as I reached up and cradled his cheek with my palm.

"Tiffany..." He turned his head until his lips brushed my palm.

Neither of us spoke.

His head started to slowly lower to mine, and my breathing quickened. My gaze locked onto his lips, and I licked mine, waiting for the electricity to hum between us the moment our lips touched like it always did. My eyelids fluttered closed, and my lips parted in anticipation when my cell phone rang.

I let out a yelp and jumped.

Matt jerked back, startled.

I frowned at the caller I.D. and answered my phone. "Zoe? What's wrong?"

"Nothing is wrong. Chaz called and said Bitsy Beaumont Brimstone just had her baby... and she's asking for you."

Chapter Nineteen

"I can't believe how tiny she is." I stared at Bitsy's baby through the nursery window at the hospital, and my heart melted. Babies really were a precious gift. She looked just like her mommy.

"Aye, lass, angels from Heaven. We'll be having a couple gifts of our own pretty soon." Matt's entire face registered his excitement.

All I felt was terrified.

"Guess I'd better get in there and see what Bitsy wants." I walked down the hall towards Bitsy's room.

"Want some company?" Matt fell into step beside me.

I stopped outside her door. "No, she asked to see me, so I'll grant her that." I could hear voices inside but couldn't tell what they were saying, although the voices were growing in volume. That couldn't be good.

Matt nodded and stepped back to lean against the wall. "If ye change yer mind, I'll be right here."

I raised my hand to knock, but the door flew open.

Brimstone stared at me, his face red and flushed, then he pulled himself together and nodded once. "Ms. Eisenhower."

"Principal Brimstone." I nodded back and then stepped inside the room while Roger started talking to Matt. I left the door open a crack. It somehow made me feel better knowing Matt was right in the hall and had my back.

Bitsy's face was flushed as well, and tear-streaked. "That man is a monster." She blew her nose.

"Who?" I handed her more tissues.

"My soon-to-be ex-husband."

My jaw fell open. "You and Roger are getting divorced?"

"Yes, no, I don't know." She wailed harder.

I sat on the edge of the bed and took her hands in mine. We might not be friends, but she was a woman and new mother. My friends and I were all about empowering and supporting women, period. It didn't matter who they were.

"Why don't you tell me what happened?"

"He's sick of me already. That's what happened."

"I doubt that's true."

"I could tell right from the start that the only reason he married me was because I was pregnant with his child. His reputation means everything to him in this stuffy old town. I think he resents me now for taking away his freedom. I know he doesn't look like a Casanova, but looks can be deceiving. He very much enjoyed the single life."

"Oh, I remember." Poor Zoe would never forget after running into him by accident at The Gentleman's Club beside Adult World when he mistook her for Little Red Riding Hood and wanted to be her big bad wolf.

"That's how I got into trouble to begin with. I fell for his lines. He didn't even wait until I was out of the hospital. Now that we had the baby while married and not out of wedlock—no offense—he informed me he wants an open marriage. He wants to become swingers. Apparently, there's a whole group of couples he knows who take turns hosting parties and hooking up with each other's spouses. He used to go to parties when he was single because a single person is called a unicorn and in high demand."

I ignored the 'having a baby out of wedlock' comment because I was shocked over the rest of the information she'd revealed. I knew Brimstone had a wild side, but I never imagined he was into that lifestyle...but hey, I wasn't one to judge.

"As long as you both are happy, then what's the harm?"

"Happy?" She scowled. "He might be happy, but I'm not. I don't want to be open, or swing, and I don't even like unicorns. They freak me out. Open? That's a joke. He means open between us but secret to the town, of course. God forbid his precious reputation be tarnished."

"What are you going to do?"

"Divorce him...I think." She gave me a pleading look. "That's why I came to you. You've been divorced and you're going to raise these babies alone. I figured you're an expert in this department. Please, Tiffany, you have to help me."

I laughed out loud.

The woman was beyond offensive, and my patience was wearing thin. "I'm no expert, Bitsy. I was only married once, and he cheated on me. I came here in good faith, but yes, you are offending me. If there's nothing else, I think I'll go." I stood.

Bitsy cried harder. "I'm sorry. Please don't leave. I've never been good with words. Never had many friends, either."

I sat back down in a chair this time. "Apology accepted. Divorce is messy and hard and shouldn't be taken lightly. Do you love Roger?"

She nodded hard.

"Then talk to him. You never know how much he's willing to compromise unless you have an honest conversation. Maybe there is a way to save your marriage, if that's what you want. You have a beautiful, precious baby girl now that you share. I've seen you and Roger together. It's plain to see he married you for more than just her. He cares about you, too."

"You really think so?"

"I do."

"You know, I too have eyes. I would give anything for Roger to look at me the way Matt looks at you." Her voice was soft. "It's okay if you don't want to marry him. You can still love each other and be a family."

I was already shaking my head. "He doesn't want that. He wants it all."

"That was before. Like you said, you'll never know what he's willing to compromise on if you don't have that honest conversation." She threw my words back at me and asked, "Do you love him?"

My heart started beating out of my chest.

My attraction from the moment I met Matthew McGinnis had grown into so much more than his external gorgeous presence. He was kind and compassionate. When I talked, he really listened. He was patient and understanding. He made me feel seen and heard and safe. Even though we lived together, I missed him when he wasn't with me. I thought about him all the time. I swallowed hard as the realization set in.

The answer was yes.

I was in love with Matt...but was love enough?

I KEPT ASKING myself that question over the next two weeks, terrified to tell him how I really felt. I knew that he cared about me and wanted more, but he hadn't said he loved me, either. And I honestly didn't know if I wanted him to...

I was still afraid he would change his mind and reject me like everyone else I had loved.

I couldn't handle that from him. It was the fear of his

rejection which held me back from saying those three little words first. I would rather stay in control, protect my heart, and go our separate ways when the year is up like we'd planned.

No romance, just friends...and co-parents.

Easier said than done, today especially.

It was the first Thanksgiving without Grammy. Matt and his Stateside family were hosting Thanksgiving in the pub. He'd tried to get me to join them, but I just couldn't. The girls had tried to get me to join them as well, but I needed to be alone with my thoughts.

Even Rita had reached out.

I had a good cry and then I headed to my grandmother's storage unit. It was time. I kept a few items myself and sorted other items for various charities. But then I stumbled upon a small, firesafe box with my name on it. I brought it home with me and proceeded to stare at it for several hours.

I don't know why I was nervous about what was inside.

I put on classical music in the background—Grammy's favorite. Then I waddled to the couch with my herbal tea, comfy maternity sweatsuit, and fuzzy socks. Propping my feet on the ottoman, I set the box next to me on the couch and finally opened it.

There was a genuine pearl necklace—her birthstone and mine—that I clasped around my neck. The cool stones settled against my skin, and I felt comforted. Next, there was a fancy letter opener. I'd always seen that on her desk for as long as I could remember, even though no one wrote letters anymore and most mail was electronic these days.

Still...I would cherish it.

I picked up a picture of her holding me as a baby, and I smiled at the look of adoration on both our faces. Looking closer, I realized she was too young for that to be me. I slowly turned the picture over, and the inscription said:

Rita, my angel from above, I'll love you with all my heart forever. Love, Mommy.

Glancing back into the box, I noticed a bundle of newspaper clippings. I picked up the stack and thumbed through it. One was the story of Tabatha's husband and daughter's death in the housefire. Others were of the books she'd illustrated. Beneath that, there was a list titled: *Referrals for Rita's Housecleaning Business*, and another list titled: *Referrals for Charlie's Classic Car Restoration Business.*

They had no idea she'd been keeping tabs on them and helping them out all along.

The last item in the box was a letter addressed to me. With shaking hands, I pulled it out and began to read my grandmother's words. I would know her handwriting anywhere.

My darling Tiffany,

If you're reading this, then I must have crossed over to raise a little hell in Heaven...if I get to Heaven, that is. This old girl has made a lot of mistakes over the years that I've tried to make amends for in my own way.

One of my biggest mistakes is what I did to you.

I never should have separated you from your sister, Tabatha. Twins are special. Your grandfather only married me for my family's money. The only good thing he ever did before he died was give me my angel, Rita. I wasn't sad when he died. That might be wrong, but he wasn't a nice man.

Rita was all I had.

Charlie took her from me, and I hated him for it. He couldn't provide for her like I could, but she didn't care. She loved him. I was jealous. I forced her to choose whom she loved more, and she chose him. I shouldn't have done that. I married your grandfather for love and would have done anything for him back then, but he was cold and heartless. It made me bitter. I didn't trust men and didn't want my angel to go through what I did when Charlie left her.

I was so sure he would, but he never did.

So, I cut her off.

When they had twins, they couldn't afford it. I'm not proud of my actions, but I saw that as my chance to get my Rita back...or some version of her. The moment I saw you and your sister, I couldn't believe how much you looked like my own daughter...the daughter I had thought I'd lost forever. The first second your eyes met mine when I picked you up, you looked straight into my soul. We shared a look like the one in the picture of me holding my Rita, and I knew I had to have you if only for a little while.

I offered to take you until Rita and Charlie could afford to raise you both. Neither one of them wanted to, but they had no choice. I had good intentions at first, I promise. But the longer I raised you, the harder it got to let you go. You were all I had left, and...

It was like my Rita had come back to me.

Over the years, your parents tried to come back for you, but they didn't have the money or lawyers like I did. I felt guilty, so I helped them anonymously. I know it wasn't right, but I didn't want to share your love with anyone.

Not again.

I realize now that was wrong. Here I am leaving you alone with no family left. I know you said you would never remarry or have children, so I worry about you and hope you change your mind someday.

Children are the greatest gift of all.

I know you're probably angry at me, and I don't blame you one bit. Please forgive me for loving you too much. I was too stubborn to make amends with my angel, but it's not too late for you. My parting gift is giving you back the family I took from you. The choice is yours on whether you let them in or not. Be careful, my darling.

Don't wind up a stubborn, bitter, lonely old woman with regrets like me.

Love,
Grammy

Matt walked through the door with to-go boxes in his hands and a big smile on his face. "I brought Thanksgiving dinner to ye, lass. I hope ye are—"

I burst into tears.

He quickly set the containers down and rushed over to me. "What's wrong?" He ran his hands over my hair and face and body, looking for anything amiss.

My heart was breaking, and an important piece had died a little tonight. I couldn't breathe. How could my grandmother have done that to me? My entire life had been a lie. And now that I was pregnant with twins of my own, I couldn't imagine anyone taking one of them from me.

I cried harder and buried my face into Matt's chest.

"Come, now, love. Yer breaking me heart." He kept running his hands up and down my back, soothingly. "What can I do to help?"

I leaned back and looked up at him with tears streaming down my face. No words were necessary. He lowered his head to mine until our lips touched. It was tender and sweet and comforting. I needed him.

Anything to stop the thoughts that were tormenting me.

He seemed to sense what I needed as he gently scooped me into his arms as if I weighed nothing and carried me down the hall to my bedroom. He laid me carefully on the bed, kissing my face and neck as he undressed me with ease.

I opened my eyes and hesitated, feeling insecure for the first time in my life. But then I saw the look in his sizzling blue eyes as he worshipped every inch of me.

"You're absolutely breathtaking," he said with a deep, husky rumble as he laid both palms on the sides of my belly.

I covered his hands with my own, suddenly not embarrassed anymore. He made me feel like a goddess. "Matt, please..."

Suddenly, his hands and mouth and tongue were everywhere at once, leaving me with no thoughts but pleasure. I tipped my head back, my eyelids fluttered closed as I orgasmed, my body seizing with delicious aftershocks. I felt him roll me onto my side, then slide into bed behind me. Spooning me, he ran his hands over my breasts, lightly pinching my sensitive nipples, and I felt myself stirring once more.

Running his palm over my stomach in a gentle caress, he kept going until he reached the apex of my thighs. He lifted my leg up over his and slid deep inside me from behind while his fingers rounded my hip and parted my folds until he found the nub of my desire. He tweaked, pressed, and made circular motions to the rhythm of his thrusts until I was squirming and moaning and crying out his name in ecstasy.

We stayed connected as he pulled the covers up over us then wrapped his arm around me with his hand cradling my belly. Maybe Bitsy was right. Maybe things could be different. Maybe I really could have it all. That was the last thought that drifted through my mind as I fell into a deep, calm, blissful, restorative sleep....

Until it wasn't.

Chapter Twenty

I gasped and sat straight up in bed naked, cold...alone.

Pain sliced through my belly, stealing my breath. It felt like I was being sliced in two. "Matt!" I screamed when I could finally breathe again.

Silence.

I began to cry. Where was he?

I scooted toward the edge of the bed when my leg brushed something wet. Oh, God, did my water break? No, no, no...it was too soon. With shaking hands, I lifted the sheet and cried out over what I saw.

Blood.

Another pain tore through me. I screamed Matt's name again as loud as I could. Still nothing. He'd left me, just like I knew he would. I needed him, and he was gone. The moment I'd let down my walls and welcomed him into my arms, he didn't want me anymore. I had dared to believe that for once, I was enough.

This rejection hurt the worst.

If I lost my babies, it was all my fault.

I never should have broken my own rule. No romance. I would never forgive myself...or him. I managed to get to the edge of the bed. The sun wasn't even up yet. Where was my phone? I tried to stand and fell to the floor, still naked and terrified. I was going to lose my babies and bleed to death.

Once more, pain ripped through me, this one the hardest. I screamed for all I was worth until it passed. Then I heard a noise from the living room. A door opening. Footsteps. I didn't care who it was. I needed help.

"Help me, please," I managed to say.

"Tiffany? Oh, you poor dear," Mrs. Cartright appeared in my bedroom. She hurried over to me and grabbed a blanket from the bed, draping it over my shivering body. "Matt gave me the security code to get inside in case he was gone, and you ever needed anything." She stood and headed to my door.

"Don't leave me like he did." I cried harder. "Please, I'm afraid."

Her kind faded brown eyes filled with compassion. "I'm not going anywhere, honey. I'm calling 911."

The next couple of hours were a blur.

Officer Pickles, Fire Chief Monroe, and Dr. Joy arrived at the same time as the ambulance. It was a small town, after all. When an emergency happened, everyone banded together to help.

Dr. Joy insisted on riding in the ambulance with me, monitoring my vitals and assessing the situation. I didn't understand half of what she said. All I knew was that I was on pain meds and half out of it, but finally pain free and resting in a private room.

Dr. Joy walked into my room and smiled. "How's my favorite patient?"

"Afraid." I pressed my lips together, waiting for her news.

"Don't be." She squeezed my hand. "Where's Matt?"

"I have no clue," was all I said, and she nodded once, no judgement or prying as usual.

I was thankful for that right now.

"Well, I can put your mind at ease." She scanned her charts. "Your big, beautiful boys are stable."

"Y-You mean I didn't lose them?" Tears leaked from my eyes and trickled down my cheeks as my heart ached with love for them.

"I'll admit, things were touch-and-go for a while there. You were in early labor and lost a lot of blood, but we managed to stop the labor and the bleeding."

"We?"

"Dr. Anderson is one of the best physicians I've ever met."

I nodded. Chaz. I owed him everything. "What caused this to happen?"

"Pregnancies are tricky with twins to begin with. I'm guessing the fall you took when the fire broke out in your spa caused trauma. Did anything happen last night that might have affected that trauma?"

I squeezed my eyes shut for a moment. "Matt and I had sex." I wanted to say made love, but he didn't love me. He couldn't have because he left me.

She looked pensive. "Normally, sex is very safe for a pregnant woman, but in your case with the recent trauma, it might have triggered early labor. I would suggest abstaining from intercourse or anything remotely stimulating until the babies are born."

"Oh, you don't have to worry about that." I raised my chin a notch and forced the tears to stay at bay.

Of course, Bud was at the root of this incident. I wanted to blame Matt for his part, but it wasn't all his fault. I'd needed him after Grammy's letter. He'd complied, no questions asked, but then he left me alone to deal with the consequences....

That hurt more than I could say.

Steeling my resolve to never let someone hurt me again, I asked. "So, what does this mean going forward? Bedrest?"

"Not necessarily total bedrest, but I don't want you doing anything that might trigger labor again. That includes extremely emotional situations. Try to stay calm and still as much as possible, okay?"

"Okay."

"Good." She nodded. "I intend to keep a close eye on you from here on out."

"I won't complain about that." I watched Dr. Joy leave and closed my eyes, exhausted. What a difference twenty-four hours could make.

A knock sounded.

"Come in," I said with my eyes still closed, too weary to open them.

"I'm here, lass," said a deep baritone voice that pierced straight through my heart.

I opened my eyes and stared at him. "You're late," I managed past the lump in my throat.

He wore the same clothes he had from the evening before as if he'd rolled out of bed after making love with me, dressed, and left as quickly as possible. Had he really needed to get away from me that badly that he couldn't even change his clothes?

"I know. I'm so sorry. I was a little preoccupied with a problem at me pub." His eyes were full of regret.

I looked away. "Well, *I* was a little preoccupied saving our babies."

"I know. I can't believe what happened. The timing was horrible." He set some flowers on my bedside stand. "These are for ye."

I stared at him. "You honestly think that makes up for what you did? You left me alone and vulnerable. I needed you, Matt. I called out for you, but you weren't there when I needed you most."

He looked like he didn't know what to say. "Ye were sleeping so peacefully; I didn't want to wake ye."

"So, you left me." I gaped at him. "You know how I feel about being rejected. Not wanted."

He scrubbed a hand over his face. "I didn't leave ye on purpose, lass. I would never do that." His gaze held mine. "Can't ye see I love ye?"

Now? He finally says the words now...after everything that happened?

I was already shaking my head. "I don't believe you." My voice hitched. I couldn't believe him. I couldn't risk my heart. I cleared my throat and said with resolve, "We made love, and I woke up needing you, but you were gone. That is a mistake I will never make again." Tears filled my eyes, and my breathing grew choppy. "You left me, Matt. I'll never forgive you for that."

His eyes grew suspiciously shiny, and he looked like he was in as much pain as I was. "Don't ye even want to hear what happened?"

"No." I turned away. "It doesn't matter."

Deep in my brain I knew I sounded unfair. Irrational. But I couldn't help it. I'd been hurt too many times in the past not to assume the worst. I couldn't go through that again.

"I think it's best if you stay on your side of the house and stop trying to take care of me. It will hurt far less that way when you don't."

"Okay, love, whatever ye want," he said, his voice full of emotion as he walked out of my room and softly closed the door behind him.

"This *is* what I want," I firmly stated as I stared at the door, regaining control.

Yes, we had agreed upon rules for a reason. This mama would protect her heart and her boys at all costs going forward. This horribly, scary incident had brought it all home.

"My boys." I smiled, placing my hands on my belly as I felt their synchronized gymnastics. I giggled and looked up expectantly at the door, instantly missing Matt's larger-than-life energy. I sniffed, and whispered into the engulfing silence of my room, this time to convince myself once and for all, "It *is* what I want."

Then why did it hurt so badly?

ONE WEEK later I went home from the hospital. Matt was absent as I requested. I hadn't spoken to him except for the text I sent, asking him to give me the afternoon to get settled back home. He said, *Okay*, and that was it.

"I really appreciate you taking me home. Both of you." I smiled at Rita and Tabatha. "You both being there for me in my time of need means more than you'll ever know."

Rita propped pillows around me on the couch. "I'm just grateful you reached out to me." She smiled at me lovingly. "I honestly never thought I would see this day."

"Almost losing my own babies gave me a new perspective on life...and family." I looked at my mother and sister. "I want us to start over if that's okay."

"I know all about what it's like to lose the things you love most," Tabatha said quietly as she sat down beside me. "I'm done with the losing part. It's time we gained something, dammit. We've all earned at least that much."

"And then some." I laughed.

"Can I ask what changed your mind?" Rita brought me some tea.

"Thank you, but you don't have to wait on me." I took the cup and warmed my hands.

"I've waited forty years to take care of my other daughter. Please don't deny me that." She covered my legs with a blanket.

My eyes grew misty. "If I'm being honest, I've waited a lifetime to be taken care of by you. It feels wonderful."

"So, about my question," she prodded gently. "Why exactly did you change your mind about letting us into your life?"

I sighed. "Grammy."

Rita blinked. "I don't understand."

Tabatha scowled. "I don't really care."

"Open that box on the end table, and you just might." I pointed to the fire-safe box I'd found in Grammy's storage unit.

Rita folded her hands in her lap and stared, looking terrified, at the box. "I-I can't."

"I can." Tabatha grabbed the box and yanked it open. Her bravado left and a look of confusion crossed her face as she sorted through the items. Her expressive face revealed all of her emotions as her throat worked to get out, "She kept tabs on me all along?"

I nodded. "She was as proud of you as she was me."

Tabatha was tougher than me. She never cried. One big tear spilled over her eyelashes and rolled down her cheek. She quickly swiped it away. "I always wondered if she knew or even cared that she had a granddaughter."

I reached out and held her hand. "She even set up a college scholarship in your daughter's name at Mayflower High School for one lucky senior each year."

"I never knew." Tabatha wiped away another tear.

I shook my head. "None of us did."

"I don't understand any of this." Rita stared at the lists of clients she'd secretly sent to her and Charlie. "She ruined my life, or tried to, but I wouldn't let her. Why would she then try to help us? My only regret in this world is in not fighting harder to keep you. We might not have had much, but we had each other."

I reached into the box and pulled out the letter. "She knew she was wrong. She had regrets but didn't know how to make amends other than giving things. That was the only world she knew."

Rita took the letter from me and read it silently. One tear grew to dozens that soaked her cheeks. "So much unnecessary pain. So much time wasted. I'm angry and frustrated and sad. I loved my mother very much. She took that away from me, too. I don't know how to process all this. How to feel."

I nodded. "It took me a while. I've been over that box

time and again, trying to sort out the enigma of Grammy. I was furious with her at first, but then I began to understand her. She's a product of what she's been through. Her strict parents, her deceitful ex, her fierce love of you and the lengths she went to keep it. She was lonely and afraid she would have nothing left without you."

"It didn't have to be that way. She could have had all of us. If only she had talked to me about how she was feeling instead of giving me ultimatums and cutting me off." Rita shook her head sadly.

"One good thing came of all this." Tabatha looked at us both. "We're a family again. I have my sister back and closure about Grammy. I can live with that."

"You're right." Rita dried her tears and nodded. "I've always felt there is no good that comes from dwelling on old hurts from the past. Sometimes we just have to let that go. The only way to true happiness is to focus on the future. Manifest what you want to happen and move forward, not back."

"That's exactly what I'm doing," I said firmly, thinking of Matt.

"Are you?" Tabatha asked.

"Yes, why do you doubt that?" I frowned.

She shrugged. "I might be overstepping my bounds, given how we just rekindled our relationship, so you might not want to hear this."

"Please, be candid with me. I'm tired of people tiptoeing around my feelings or not being honest with me. Say what you have to say. I won't get mad."

"I think you're so focused on your past that you won't give Matt a chance to be in your future. Don't let Bud take anything else from you."

"What does Bud have to do with this?" The first seed of doubt settled deep into my gut, telling me I might have overreacted with Matt.

"Let's just say I'm finally putting myself out there. I spent the evening with Police Chief LaLone, and I heard the call come in over his radio. Bud broke into McGinny's Pub and stole money while his new girlfriend was setting up a space heater in his back room."

My face paled. "How did I not hear this?"

"You were in the hospital, dear," Rita said.

"That must have been what he was trying to explain to him when I said it didn't matter why he left me, and then I made him leave my room." How had I misjudged him so unfairly? Because like Grammy I had been trained to assume the worst rather than give the benefit of doubt and be let down.

"Matt's secret alarm went off, and he got to his pub just in time to put the fire out," Tabatha went on. "He has Bud and his girl on security footage, but they got away with the day's cash before they could be caught. Matt spent hours working with Officer Pickles on filing a report. As soon as they find Bud, he will get exactly what he deserves. He won't see the light of day for years to come."

"And he won't be after your money anymore," Rita added firmly. "Matt's private investigator is a friend of your father's. He has enough footage proving Bud is a fraud and has no physical limitations whatsoever."

"What am I going to do?" I asked. "I've made such a mess of things."

"Talk to him. Tell him how you feel." Rita hugged me. "Honesty is always the best policy, and Tabatha is right. We've all wasted far too much time."

"After everything I said, I'm not sure Matt will want to talk to me."

"Here's an idea. Grammy was on to something, she just waited far too long to execute it." Tabatha grabbed a pad of paper and pen from the kitchen counter and handed them to me. "Write him a note and leave it in his room. He can read it when he gets back. It's actually kind of romantic."

I nodded. "That I can do. I journal all the time. I'll just pretend that's what I'm doing. Thank you both again so much. If you don't mind, I would like to be alone with my thoughts so I can write this before he gets back this evening."

"Good luck, sweetheart." Rita kissed my cheek. "You know where we are if you need us."

Tabatha hugged me. "Call Mom if you need anything. I have a second date." She winked. We all laughed, and then they left.

I spent the next thirty minutes writing down everything I felt. My hopes, my fears, my love for him. How I wanted it all and was going to tell him that morning, but then the unthinkable happened. I went into early labor and panicked then blamed everything on him, terrified he didn't love me back and wanting to be the one to push him away first.

I glanced at the clock. I'd only told him to give me a few hours. He would be home soon, and this would be the first I had seen him in the week since I was in the hospital. Inhaling a deep breath, I headed down the hall to his bedroom. With shaking hands, I opened his door and stepped inside. My jaw fell open. Matt wasn't just gone...

He had moved out.

Chapter Twenty-One

Another week later, it was girls' night at my ranch, mostly because the girls didn't want me going anywhere. They also wouldn't let me cook. They showed up with a sub tray, chips, fruit bowl, vegetable tray, and drinks. We brought the party to my living room and enormous sectional couch so I could put my feet up.

"I feel like such a slacker." I sipped club soda. It was the only thing that settled my stomach.

Now that I was in the last trimester, I could only eat small amounts, so I was hungry all the time. Indigestion and heartburn were real. I barely got anything down and it came right back up. There was literally no room in my stomach from the two bear cubs squishing everything. Don't even get me started on my bladder. Every time I stood, I had to go.

"You're not supposed to do anything but rest, hon.

Doctor's orders, remember?" Zoe took my nearly full plate from me and set it on an end table.

"How could I forget." I sighed.

"I'm glad you made up with your mom and sister." Morticia sipped her diet cola. "I'd give anything to talk to my mother again. Can't exactly talk to my father about his new girlfriend who's my age, and I don't have a sister."

"You have us, babe." Harmony patted her on the back.

"I know, and I love you girls." Morti shrugged. "It just would be nice to have more family. Or create my own."

"It is nice," I said. "I have to admit, I'm getting excited for the boys to arrive. Terrified, but excited."

"Speaking of the boys...how are things with Matt?" Zoe sipped her chardonnay, studying me carefully.

"Not good." I stirred the straw around the lime in my club soda. "I can't believe he moved out. Like without even talking about it. It doesn't make sense. That's totally out of character for him."

"Maybe he has a good reason. You *did* tell him that you didn't believe he loved you, and that whatever he had to say didn't matter," Morti said. "Then you asked him to stay on his half of the house and leave you alone. I'd say he took you literally."

"Yes, but after I found out what happened, I realized I had rushed to judgement. I wrote him that letter explaining everything I couldn't bring myself to say. How can I give that to him when he won't take my calls?"

"Wait, he won't answer you?" Harm asked, incredulously. "What about his responsibility for his boys?"

As much as I appreciated her defense of me, I had to be honest.

"He always texts me back and asks if something is wrong with the boys. When I say no, he has nothing else to say to me. I asked him if he would come over so we could talk. He said he was busy with something very important and had to go. He is always there for his boys, but apparently, not for me."

"Well..." Morti started to say.

"I know, I know. It's all my fault. He is only giving me exactly what I wanted. Except, that's no longer what I want."

"What exactly do you want, Tiff?" Harm asked.

"I want it all," I threw up my hands, "but I have no idea how to get it."

"You've always been resourceful, hon," Zoe said. "I believe in you. You'll think of something."

"You know what?" I said. "You're right, doll. Matthew McGinnis ordered me to marry him. Then he bulldozed his way into my life, taking over buying and decorating for the twins. He insisted on taking care of me and going to all of my doctor appointments. Then suddenly I'm supposed to know that he loves me? He never told me. He just expected me to know and then moved out when I didn't believe him. I'm good at expressing myself. I was just afraid to. He's not afraid to say how he feels. He's just not very good at it."

"Dude, what are you going to do?" Harm rubbed her hands together.

"I'm going to show him what a *real* proposal looks like." I nodded.

"No way," Morti said. "You're actually going to propose to him?"

"I am. I'll need a ring, lots of ribbon with a big bow, and a cute outfit...or as cute as maternity clothes can be."

"I'll get the ring. I have plenty of brothers with hands as big as Matt who can help me find something masculine and perfect for McShamrock." Harm nodded.

"We have plenty of shiny silver ribbons and bows at the funeral home, so I've got that covered." Morti made a note.

"And I can certainly pick out a maternity outfit you'll look lovely in, hon," Zoe chimed in.

"Perfect. Christmas is in two weeks," I said, getting excited. "I plan to put a gift under the tree he can't refuse."

"How are you going to get him over there?" Harm asked.

"I'm not. You girls are."

"And how are we going to do that?" Morti added.

"Well, he already surprised me the other day when I wasn't home but putting up a tree and hanging lights outside. I have Grammy's old angel she used to put on our tree every year. This will be my first Christmas without her. I feel like if I put the angel up, a piece of her will be with me. When the time is right, tell him I plan to put the angel on the top of the tree myself because I don't want to bother him. That will get him there. And when he arrives, he'll find me in his stocking."

"What if he says no?" Zoe asked gently.

"That's not an option." I shook my head. "I can't live without him, even if he might be part of some crazy clover cult. I'll show him he doesn't need that or anything else because I am enough."

"Damn straight you are, babe. We all are." Harm raised a glass. "To us."

We all said "Cheers," and took a sip of our drinks, then got to work on Mission Shamrock.

THE NEXT TWO weeks flew by.

The girls pulled off their parts of the plan perfectly. Harmony's oldest brother owned a jewelry store and was a regular at McGinny's Pub. He could tell just by looking at Matt's hands what size his ring finger was. He ordered a traditional Claddagh Ring in solid gold. It featured a design of two hands holding a heart, topped with a crown. The ring symbolized love from the heart, friendship from the lands, and loyalty from the crown.

It was perfect.

Next, Morticia found the perfect smooth and silky, shiny gold ribbon and bows from the supply closet at Smith's Funeral Home. They made many floral arrangements, depending on the type of service their clients wanted. I ignored the fact that the arrangements were usually made for the dearly departed, and chose to imagine they were now serving the dearly beloved.

I could live with that.

Finally, Zoe found the most stunning white maternity dress I had ever seen. I didn't even know they made something like this, and I knew fashion. It had silky fabric, a plunging neckline, long flowy sleeves, and hugged my belly just enough to be flattering and make me look less like I was wearing a tent.

The part I loved the most was the matching satin slippers with fuzzy white accents.

Everything was set. Matt had taken a trip back to Ireland to celebrate the holiday early with his family, but he was due home this morning. His uncle was picking him up at the airport. In typical small-town fashion, the citizens all knew about the plan at this point, and they highly approved, even if my methods were unorthodox.

The mayor joked he would expect nothing less from me.

Meanwhile, I was so nervous. I got ready, slipping the ring and the letter in a hidden pocket in my dress. The girls cleaned my place, set classical mood music, lit the fireplace, dimmed the lights, and set out sparkling grape juice and strawberries.

"You look beautiful." Zoe blinked back tears.

"Are you sure?" I bit my bottom lip.

"You're always beautiful, Tiff." Morti gave me her rare Mona Lisa smile.

"Thank you, ladies, so much. I couldn't have done any of this without you."

"It's time, babe," Harm said.

"Oh, God." I swallowed hard.

"You'll be fine. You've got this." Zoe hugged me followed by the other two.

"I'll text you when Matt is on his way." Harm led the way out the door, and then they were gone.

I couldn't sit still, so I stood and paced. My stomach twinged, and I rubbed the spot, crooning softly to my babies. It was so strange to me how I already felt like a mother after thirty-two weeks. They hadn't even been born, yet I felt like I already knew them and loved them unconditionally.

I now realized my mother had given me to my grandmother because she would do anything for her children. She thought she was doing what was best for me. I also now knew my grandmother had done the same in her own way, as wrong as that may be.

I'd learned to forgive and let go of the past.

It was freeing.

I was working on letting go of what Bud had done to me, and proposing to Matt was the first step. He was everything that Bud wasn't, and I deserved to be happy. No more being afraid. No more hiding behind walls. No more denying my feelings.

I was in love with Matthew McGinnis, and it was time he knew.

The doorknob at the front door jiggled, and I jumped. He was here. Smoothing a hand down the front of my dress, I rushed over to greet him. Opening the door, I smiled wide...but then my smile vanished.

"Bud?" I'd never seen him so unkempt and disheveled. "What are you doing here? You know what, I don't care. The answer is no. Get out." I started to shut the door, but he stuck his foot in the way and barged in.

"You ruined my life, you bitch." His face twisted with rage. "I want what's mine. Give me money, or I'll make you pay like you have me." He took a menacing step toward me. "I can't go to jail. I would never survive."

I stumbled back a few steps. "I didn't do anything to you. You did it to yourself. Trying to burn down my spa. Stealing from Matt and trying to burn down his pub. What is wrong with you? You're not acting like yourself." He'd made bad decisions in the past, like starting a business that failed, and then losing a fortune gambling, but this time he looked different. "Are you high?"

"Shut up." He shoved me until my back hit the wall, and I gasped.

"You're hurting me." I carefully covered my stomach with my hands. "What do you want?"

"Money and your car keys. Give me my share, and I'll leave the country. You'll never see me again."

"Yer damn right she won't, because ye won't be around to see anything, laddy." Matt's voice was deep and deadly.

Bud whirled around to face Matt, and I slipped away from the wall and dialed 911. His eyes were crazy and glazed over as he stared down Matt. "You're not so tough. You're all talk. A big, dumb primate. I box." He held up his fists.

"I bite." Matt snapped his teeth.

Bud's fists slipped. "You're a gold digger."

Matt sneered, baring his teeth. "Yer as fake as yer bad back."

Sirens wailed in the distance, and Bud made a run for the door.

Matt grabbed him by the jacket, and Bud turned around then punched Matt in the chest hard. "Self-defense, laddy. Thank ye fer that." Matt chuckled deeply, his grin coming slow and sweet. "Time to go night-night. Lights out." With one blow to Bud's face that didn't even look that hard, Bud tumbled to the floor in an unconscious heap just as Officer Pickles arrived.

The next hour was spent arresting Bud and his girl-friend, who was dumb enough to have stayed in the getaway car out front. Matt and I both gave our statements, and finally, the police left. My nerves were shot.

Bud has always been a nuisance, but he'd never been dangerous. He had to be addicted to drugs. That explained why he was so desperate for money this time. I was just glad that part of my life was finally over, and I refused to let my past dictate my future.

I would not let Bud win.

"This is not how I had planned on tonight going." I looked down at my wrinkled outfit and messed-up hairdo. No matter what it took, I was going to salvage this night.

Matt looked at me as if just now recognizing how I was dressed. His gaze ran around the room, pausing on the sparkling grape juice and strawberries. He looked back at me. "Wow, that's quite a dress fer hanging an angel on a tree."

"I have plans tonight...after."

His brow puckered and then narrowed. "I see. With anyone I know?"

"I'm pretty sure you've heard of him." I winked. "He's a legend."

His eyes widened. "Tiffany, what is this?"

I started to lower myself to one knee and thought better of it.

Matt grabbed my arm before I could fall.

"Matthew McGinnis, you are the most stubborn man I know." I still held onto his arms.

He arched a brow. "I believe the proper thing to say is *thank ye*."

"Let me finish, Sasquatch."

He kept his lips zipped, but they tipped up slightly at the corners. My heart fluttered, and I cleared my throat. I needed to get this out. This man, who'd grown to be so important to me in such a small amount of time needed to hear what was in my heart.

"You are also the kindest, most gentle and understanding man I know."

"I try." He shrugged, and I swear I saw a wee bit of pink tinting his face.

I distracted the butterflies in my stomach by sliding my hands down his rock-solid arms and weaving my fingers with his. I glanced down at how perfectly they fit together.

We were a perfect fit.

My gaze drifted up until my eyes met his. Swallowing the ball of nerves suddenly lodged in my throat, I said, "I'm sorry for everything I said in the hospital. I didn't mean it."

His gaze softened. "I know."

My eyes sprang wide. "You do?"

He nodded.

"Do you know I love you, too?"

"I have fer a while." His thumbs stroked the backs of my hands, and his gentle smile warmed every part of me.

I blinked. "Well, this was easier than I thought." My own smile grew bigger as excitement for our future took hold. "I changed my mind. I want it all."

"I was counting on that." His eyes twinkled with mischief and love, and I couldn't hold myself back any longer.

"Matthew Michael McGinnis, will you marry me?"

"No."

I sucked in a sharp breath. "No?"

"I can't say *yes* right—"

And just like that my water broke.

Chapter Twenty-Two

"That's it, Tiffany, push one more time for me," Dr. Joy said. "Don't hold back. Give it all you've got."

As the contraction grew to its peak, I pushed hard and screamed harder. "I hate you, Matthew McGinnis."

"I know, love, it's okay." He held my hand and didn't let go even when I dug my fingernails into him.

"I see the head. You're doing great," Dr. Joy said as the contraction passed. "When the next one comes, I want you to push as hard as you can, okay? I think this one will be the one to push him out."

"Okay." I'd been at this for hours.

I'd spent half the night yelling, crying, and screaming at Matt. I hated him. I loved him. I didn't want to ever see him again. I didn't want him to ever leave my side. Through it all he kept rubbing my forehead with a cool washcloth and holding my hand and massaging my back and walking me around the room, taking whatever I dished out.

We didn't speak of him turning down my proposal.

I was in too much pain of another kind.

I stared at the spot and focused on my breathing like I'd been taught with Matt during Lamaze classes. "Oh, God, here comes another one." I gripped his hand once more and started pushing hard.

"Push from your abdomen, not your face," Dr. Joy instructed. "You're going to break blood vessels in your eyes and that won't help your baby enter this world."

I concentrated on what she said and ignited my core like I had back in our cheerleading days. I was a strong woman. I could do this. Pushing with all my might, I suddenly felt a whoosh and then no more pain.

The whole room grew silent for a moment until a strong cry pierced the air.

Matt whooped, and I cried, while Dr. Joy cleaned the baby off and set him on my chest where he settled in peaceful and quiet. He was a big boy for two months early. In that instant, I fell in love like I had never loved anything before.

He was utter perfection.

I looked up at Matt, and he was crying. He touched the baby's face, and then leaned down and kissed me on the lips. I guess I didn't have to have it all to be happy, I thought, but the ache in my chest grew.

"Can we call him Declan after me Da?"

"That sounds perfect."

My mind snapped back into focus when another contraction hit me. Dr. Joy handed the baby to a nurse to tend to.

"Okay, mama, let's focus on bear cub number two." She gave me a slight smile.

I gave her a slight laugh. She'd heard me say that hundreds of times referring to the boys. My laughter died when another contraction came on faster and harder. My body shook. This baby felt like he was twisting and turning and kicking his way into the world. I would have thought the second child would be easier.

I cursed and screamed and yelled at Matt again.

And once again, he took it all in stride.

He really was the most patient human being I knew. I went through the series of pushing once more, and finally, blessedly, the baby was born kicking and screaming into the world, much smaller than the first, yet packing a far bigger punch.

The whole room erupted with everyone talking at once.

"What's wrong?" I grabbed Matt's hand.

"Nothing, love, except...we have a daughter." He smiled through his tears.

"What? How?" I looked at Dr. Joy.

She held up her hands. "What can I say? Sometimes the sex is hard to determine for sure, especially with twins. They tend to hide behind each other. Consider yourself lucky." She handed me my daughter.

I took one look at her face, and my heart melted over

my own little spitfire. She looked exactly like Grammy. I knew she would find a way even in death to still be in my life and make me forgive her.

Eugenia. I looked at Matt. "Can we call her Genie?"

"That sounds about perfect to me, love." He kissed her forehead, and my heart cracked wide open.

It felt like a whirlwind. Matt went to freshen up as the babies were tended to, as well as myself. By the time I was settled into my own room with both babies in a basinet beside me, Matt had returned. He looked so handsome. Freshly showered and wearing a shirt and tie tucked into his standard jeans.

He'd never looked better.

He set a bouquet of roses on my bedside table, his dimples sinking deep as he smiled at me. "Hi, lass."

"Hi yourself."

"Ye did good, Mammy." His gorgeous blue eyes blazed with pride.

"I did, didn't I?" I nodded, feeling damn proud of myself.

His face grew serious. Nervous, even. He cleared his throat. "We have a conversation we never got to finish back at our house."

So now it was *our* house again? "Oh, I don't know. It stopped being our house when you moved out, and we were pretty much over when you said no."

"Ah, but I did not just say no. I said I can't say *yes* right...and then yer water broke."

"Okay, then finish what you were going to say." I felt

fearless now. No more nerves for me. After birthing two babies, I felt like I could do anything.

"I meant I can't say *yes* right now. Or, then as it was."

"You said you loved me."

"Aye."

"And do you still?"

"More than ever."

"Then why can't you marry me?"

"I can now."

"I'm confused."

"For the record, I proposed first, ye know."

"You demanded. And then I proposed."

"You tried, but I had to stop ye."

"Again, why?"

"Because I had planned on proposing again."

"You did?"

"You were right, love." His eyes filled with emotion. "Words are cheap. I moved out because ye were right not to believe me. I needed to show ye that I loved ye more than life itself. I told ye I was busy with something important, and I was." His eyes twinkled. "Why do you think I went to Ireland?"

"To see your family for an early Christmas."

"True, but while I was there, I got me Grammy's gold Celtic Knot ring."

I blinked back tears. "You did?"

"Aye, I did." He pulled out the ring which consisted of a beautiful blue sapphire and two Celtic knots on each side. "Tiffany Rose Eisenhower, will ye make me the happiest man alive and marry me?"

"Yes! Today, tomorrow, always." Tears streamed down my face as he slipped the ring on my finger. "I really do love you so much." He kissed me softly, and my heart was full for the first time in my life. "You know, I had Harmony's older brother order you a gold Claddagh ring."

"Ye did?" Matt looked surprised.

"You didn't think I would propose without a ring, did you?"

His eyes filled with love. "That's me favorite kind."

"It was in the pocket of my dress when my water broke. Can you get it for me?"

My dress was with my belongings in the corner of the room. He found the ring and his hand paused. "What's this?" He stared at the letter I had written him.

"That's what I have been trying to give you ever since you moved out and I realized I couldn't live without you."

He slowly opened the letter and read in silence then walked over and kissed me softly on the lips. "Ye'll never have to live a day without me again, love."

I took the ring box from him and opened the case as I looked him in the eyes. "Will you wear this for me?"

"I would be honored." He smiled with pride as I slid it on his finger.

Just then Declan started crying for once instead of Genie.

"Can you bring him to me? His diaper probably needs

to be changed. Better do it before the girls arrive. They can't wait to see our babies."

"Sure thing." Matt gently lifted the baby from the basinet, careful not to disturb little Genie. He set Declan on my lap on the bed.

"You're probably better at this than I am with all the experience from your nieces and nephews."

"I have changed a few nappies in me time. No worries, love. I'll walk ye through it."

I bit my bottom lip in concentration over my very first diaper change. Undoing the tape at the sides, I peeled back the diaper and grabbed the wet wipes. When I looked back at my son, I gasped. My gaze lifted to my fiancé, finally understanding the legend of the clover.

"That's not a tattoo after all." I laughed.

"Aye, it's a family birthmark to a lucky few." He winked.

"I'm lucky you're not part of a cult." I sighed in relief.

"You are one strange lass, me love." He chuckled. "I love it."

"And I love you, my lucky charm." I kissed him soundly on the mouth.

Everything melded in this moment. Him, me, our babies, and our future. So much love in one small hospital room. I'd never felt happier or more blessed. All because I was afraid to turn forty. One thing was sure...

I'd do it all again.

Books By Kari Lee Townsend

<u>KALLI BALLAS MYSTERY</u>

Mind Over Murder

Two Cents of Doom

A Touch of Malice

An Inkling of Evil

Mayhem on the Mind

<u>CECE MONROE MYSTERY</u>

Harmful Habits

<u>SUNNY MEADOWS MYSTERY</u>

Tempest in the Tea Leaves

Corpse in the Crystal Ball

Trouble in the Tarot

Shenanigans in the Shadows

Perish in the Palm

Hazard in the Horoscope

Chaos and Cold Feet

Murder in the Meditation

Cruising into Danger

Road Trip to Ruin

<u>DIGITAL DIVA</u>

Talk to the Hand

Rise of the Phenoteens

Books By Kari Lee Harmon

COLDWATER COVE

Dark Seas

Frozen Waters

Dangerous Thaw

Deadly Frost

STANDALONE NOVELS

Valley of Secrets

Until Tomorrow

Project Produce

Love Lessons

LAKEHOUSE TREASURES NOVELLAS

James

Amber

Meghan

Brook

MERRY SCROOG-MAS NOVELLAS

Naughty or Nice

Sleigh Bells Ring

Jingle all the Way

TRIPLE R RANCH SHORT STORIES

Destiny Wears Spurs

Spurred by Fate

Portrait of a Woman

Resilient

Resourceful

About the Author

Kari Lee Townsend is a National Bestselling Author of mysteries & a tween superhero series. She also writes romance and women's fiction as Kari Lee Harmon. With a background in English education, she's now a full-time writer, wife to her own superhero, mom of 3 sons, 1 darling diva, 1 daughter-in-law & 2 lovable fur babies. These days you'll find her walking her dogs or hard at work on her next story, living a blessed life.